DARK TALES – VOLUME 2

I0683005

Edited by Dorothy Davies

DARK TALES – VOLUME 2

GRAVESTONE PRESS

TABLE OF CONTENTS

Necrotic Epiphany (Paul Edwards)

Eyes like cigarette burns. Black hair streaked with green dye, hanging in scraggly ribbons. Dr Freudstein, the undead surgeon from *The House by the Cemetery*, reaches out a bony hand on his chest.

Natalie skips and flits across the dance floor to sit beside him on a bench. *"The House by the Cemetery* rocks!" she says, nodding at his T-shirt.

He flashes her a smile. "Yeah... although I prefer *The Beyond.*" He slots a Marlboro between his lips. "You got a light?"

"Sure," she says, fumbling for her lighter in her jacket pocket. She whips it out and sparks up his cigarette. "Nothing beats the intestine spew in *City of the Living Dead,* right?"

The smile returns to his lips. "Name's Alex."

"Natalie."

They shake hands, beads and charms chattering around his wrist.

He's so handsome, she thinks.

The DJ spins *This Corrosion* by The Sisters of Mercy and the Goth-kids with their bone-white faces and kohl-streaked eyes fill up the entire dance floor.

Alex tucks a flap of black hair behind his ear. "So, you live near here?"

"Ten minutes away. It's an old place. Used to be a Methodist church."

He nods absently, his gaze flickering around the club. "And you're alone?"

"Oh, don't worry," she smiles, touching the pentagram on a chain around her neck. "I'm more than capable of looking after myself, you know."

***

Alex moves to the window, rubbing condensation away with the palms of his hands. On the windowsill are stacks of worm-eaten books with weird sounding titles. *Al Azif. Vodoun. Dark Moon Mysteries. Cultes des Goules. Witch's Master Grimoire.* He looks down into the weed and nettle-infested graveyard, catching the hollow stare of a crumbling stone angel.

Natalie steps out of the shadows behind him, arms wrapped around her lithe, milk-white frame. "You like me then," she says.

"Yes," he replies. "Very much so."

Something in her hand glitters and glints, reflecting the glow of the moon through the window. "But how do I *really* know that?" He turns his head only to see something sharp flash toward his throat. "They're only words," she says, cutting deep, slicing true, "and words alone mean nothing."

***

Her boy.

Her lover.

Her sweet, adorable Alex.

She likes nothing better than to hold him, to kiss him, to tell him he's all she wants and all she'll ever need.

On black, starless nights they'll curl up and watch DVDs together. Horror movies like *Tombs of the Blind Dead, The Serpent and the Rainbow, La Maschera del Demonio, The Living Dead at the Manchester Morgue, The Black Remote, Zombie Creeping Flesh.*

The five-pointed star she used in the ritual remains chalked on the floor, next to her open Book of Shadows and a box of black candles. Love potions wear off; this, she hopes, will be permanent.

Late one night she wakes to find him facing the mirror on the back of the door.

She sits up in bed, clawing her hair away from her eyes. "Alex?"

His reflection hangs in the mirror's dusty, filthy darkness. He reaches up, touching the crude stitchwork in his neck.

Natalie's heart thumps and thunders. "What?" she says. "What is it, Alex?"

"I'm not like you," he says in a low, unemotional voice. The words hang in the air and she thinks – *he can't know.*

"It's late," she says, patting the space on the mattress beside her. "Come back to bed."

He turns away from his reflection at last, shuffling obediently across the room and into her eagerly enfolding arms.

***

Natalie draws the curtains and slots *Hell of the Living Dead* into the DVD player. "This movie's a rip-off of *Dawn of the Dead,*" she says, "but it's still a pretty good watch."

9

She sits beside him on the sofa, fingers splayed out on his leg, gently squeezing and rubbing his knee. Alex, as still as a statue, stares silently at the television.

Halfway through the film she senses his eyes on her. She turns to him, smiling. She leans forward, pressing her mouth to his, feeling his cold hands clasp and then squeeze her face with their hungry fingers.

Then – pain.

Awful, searing pain.

She tears free just as Alex emits a sound which might have been a laugh, her open, now-tongueless mouth trying so hard to scream.

Alex grips her shoulders, severing her jugular with the jagged remnants of his rotted teeth. Natalie's body jerks and spasms before falling backwards through the coffee table with a loud, bone-splintering *CRASH!*

Alex chews and drools and swallows, his eyes black as pitch. He blinks slowly and stares at the living dead as they devour a young girl on TV.

A gory smile splits his face in two.

Moments later he's on his knees, his arms outstretched, his crimson-coloured hands pawing at the TV screen. Through a mouthful of blood and lumps of half-chewed flesh he groans excitedly to his kind, his own, his *kin…*

Sunday Service (Rickey Rivers Jr.)

I left for church at my usual time. On arrival I saw only one car in the parking lot, a small black compact. None of the church members had a car like that. I thought that maybe a guest had wanted to arrive first and greet the pastor.

The church doors were open. Pastor Sullivan usually opened the doors early to allow members sanctuary before service started. But his car wasn't there. I thought he must have gotten a new one.

I went into the church. It was nearly empty and cold too. A figure was crouched in the darkness, a woman with long white hair sitting in the front row. Sunlight beamed through the church windows. It seemed to touch every pew but the one she sat on. I said a small prayer and approached the stranger.

"Good morning."

She gave no answer.

I moved a bit closer and repeated my greeting. The woman was looking straight ahead. There were tears in her eyes. She was elderly. I had never seen her before. She might have been lost. I felt a pull of sadness from her direction. I apologized, and moved to leave her be.

"No," she said. "That's alright."

The woman had a certain look. It looked like she'd been crying a while, crying to herself in the dark. The shadows home to her.

"Is everything alright?" I asked.

The woman smiled. "Everything's alright."

I asked if she had wanted to join the church, or was simply a guest.

The woman hung her head. "I'm only here for the funeral."

This surprised me. Today was a regular Sunday.

"Sorry," I said. "There isn't a funeral today."

"But there is," she said and nothing else.

She cried a quiet cry. I thought that maybe she'd lost someone recently or was confused about her location. She was distraught, it made sense. In grieving times you can often be lost.

"Ma'am," I said. "I can help you find the right church, if you want me to."

I sat beside her. The pew was warm.

She shook her head. "No thank you. I'm in the right place."

I was careful with my next question, as to not offend. I asked her who she thought had passed away.

The woman turned to face me. The details in her face were like repaved roads. "You don't know?" she said. Her voice was weak, the weakened voice of child.

I thought to myself, but no one came to mind. The pastor hadn't mentioned a funeral, and our church was small. As far as I knew none of the members had passed. Furthermore, I was in service last week and there were no funeral announcements. Nothing in the church could lead anyone to believe a funeral was scheduled today. The outside church sign simply read 'All are welcome' Apparently, I was lost myself.

"Sorry," I said. "I don't know anything about a funeral."

With that, as if struck by something, the woman stood up and brought her hands together. The sound made an echo in the empty church. I somehow felt air of the clap on the back of my neck, like a small sting from an unseen bug. A smell like an old farm arose. It reminded me of a fieldtrip I took years back.

The woman prayed to herself. I waited and watched. I felt myself squeeze my knees. Her mouth was moving so fast. It was like she was speaking in a long lost tongue. She finished in seconds and turned away from me, her head moving firstly then her body. It was like someone above was twisting her. She started walking down the aisle and toward the church entrance. I was nearly bound to the pew. It took effort, but I pulled myself away from simply watching her leave. I caught up to her. My legs were heavy.

"Ma'am," I said. "I can help."

The woman turned to me, her head firstly. Twisted, her neck bent like an old rubber hose. I had angered her. I saw that clearly. I started to apologize, but my tongue stuck itself to the roof of my mouth. With tears escaping the road like curves in her face she stared almost through me. In the light of the church entrance I could see the roads of her face were worn. Her lips were cracked. Her nose was flared. Her stare was a tangible thing. Tears seemed to steam on her road like face.

I forced out a word, "Ma'am." It came out so small, as a squeak of a mouse. I could speak no further. The woman threw up both hands. Her eyes were beaming, the glare so bright it forced me backwards.

With a splitting tongue she said, "Don't follow."

And she walked away through the church doors into the Sunday morning light. I didn't physically follow her. My mind told me where she had come from. After her leave a harsh chill came into the church. It froze me. Sometime later a great relief came. The black compact car sped by in a blaze, vanishing in the morning light. I didn't realize how heavy the air had been until she left. Fresh air seemed to return itself all at once, like the doors of the church had been newly opened again.

***

I had to leave that church. I didn't feel the same going there. The encounter has stuck with me for what feels like a long time. The chill refuses to leave. At times I feel my throat drying and I'm reminded all over again.

Weeks after the encounter a terrible thing happened: there was a church fire. All the members passed away. The doors were sealed from the inside. Even the pressure of the inside flames couldn't force the church doors open. The newspaper interviewed a fireman and I remember him saying "It was like someone cast a spell on the doors." They had to break the church windows to get in.

I went to the group funeral expecting to see the woman again. I never did.

Mark My Steps (Victoria Nangle)

I look up at the familiar sound of the front door latch closing, stretching my neck to gaze over the back of the sofa towards the sound.

"Hello you!" I cry as you bring in a gust of cold air from the early evening.

"Hello back." You kiss the top of my head with a tired grin and drop yourself like a dead weight on the other end of the sofa I've been hogging. I slip my legs down to give you space and draw your feet up to my lap, as I do most evenings, pulling your worn trainers off and putting them neatly on the floor, laces still tied. Like a couple of beaten up soldiers at attention guarding the dust bunnies behind them in the darkness.

"So?"

"So what?" you tease.

"So, did you hear anything back about New York?" I tweak the toes of your left sock, holding the fabric between thumb and forefinger and pull it off in one sweep.

"No." You giggle as the cotton tickles your sole. "But, I wouldn't hold your breath."

I pull the right sock off by its collar and ball it with its mate, storing them inside a trainer.

"Okey dokey" - resolute to be bright - "so sidebar that and tell me about your day while I relax your feet." And with that I sit myself up cross legged facing you, swing the heel of the sockless foot I still have in my hand onto my left knee and start resolutely working the heels of my thumbs into

15

the knots you've picked up today. I begin with the ball of your foot.

"Well… what's that lovely smell?"

"Just dinner. I've popped all the veg into the slow cooker. We can dice some German sausage onto it to beef it up a bit when we're ready to eat. Now - your day."

"Ah yes." And I can feel the tension already loosening in your leg as you know you're home.

"As you may recall from yesterday's episode of My Life, today was stock taking day. Which Em and I totally did with professionalism and aplomb."

I look up from my kneading and raise an eyebrow sceptically.

"Well, ish." You admit. I grin and go back to the muscles in your instep. "It really doesn't take long to get half of the stuff checked and we've got two days put aside to get the whole job finished. And that left us half the day to explore the back room. It's all about familiarity with what we're selling. In the long run exploring will make us an asset to the business, having total familiarity with everything in the shop and knowing exactly where it is…"

"What have you found?!" I almost shout.

I love that you love where you work. The fact that what others see as a junk shop you delight in as a treasure trove. Even though it's owned by the same people that own these shops that take a punt on house clearances and estate sale job lots across the globe, you and Em have made this your own Aladdin's Cave of wonders. With ageing Jubilee bunting celebrating the end of its back-of-the-cupboard relegation from the ceilings and stacks of

16

issues of Punch magazine from two centuries ago piled high behind the counter for easy reach - should there be a lull in business. With this kind of intake, regular stock takes are a real treat.

"Well? What's this gem then?" I push on impatiently to your gleeful face which also might be conveying that I'm pushing a bit too hard with my knuckle around your heel. I let up on both pressures accordingly.

You smile. "It's an UpDown Horse."

Clearly your big reveal is leaving me a little nonplussed.

"A metal horse for children. Listen," you settle in. "In 1942 Mobo Toys in Kent invented the Bronco horse. Modelled on a zebra - because they went to a taxidermists for a horse model and he was all out - go figure, you'd think they might just look at some old Stubbs paintings in the National Gallery or something - ow! I'll focus!" I smirk. "So they use bicycle gears inside this metal shell that stands upright like a zebra so that when you push down on the stirrups and then release them the whole thing moves forward, with you on it. They were painted like carousel horses, with the colours chosen by children at the school near to the factory."

I make an interested face and switch feet.

"When they took them to market in the late 1940s there was also going to be a tin man too, but he never made it to the shops, which is a shame because he would've been the first Action Man maybe."

"Maybe." I agree, smiling. I love this enthusiasm and I'm imaging the colours on a painted tin Action Man from the 1940s, who might stand a bit like a zebra.

"Anyway," you continue, lying further back into the sofa cushions on your end and gazing nonchalantly at the rose moulding in the ceiling, "the Bronco horses only went forward in a straight forward line between 1947 and 1950. After that they worked out a way for leaning on one stirrup in preference over another to change direction…"

"Like a motorbike?" I ask, partly to show I'm paying attention.

"Exactly like that!" You spring up startling me and the foot I'm holding kicks me in the shin with the force of your body's movement.

"Sorry." You sit back a bit, chastened by your own exuberance. "Anyway," shifting up and facing me with your legs out in front, leaning to kiss my hurt shin lightly, "this one only goes straight and it looks awesome even with the rust and I may have sat on it and used it and made it go and it goes and up and down as it moves forward and that's why I've called it an UpDown Horse." And on your back again, as if the running sentence was the air from the balloon of you.

I start to tug your toes one by one, gently. "And knowing things like that" I say affectionately, "and finding gems like that is exactly why they're going to want you to run the New York shop," I tell you as my hands move to encompass a foot each, feeling the tension and flow of muscle, hard skin and blister prone danger areas, soft dry arches and hardworking tendons in the landscape of your feet.

"Yes. Maybe. Fingers crossed."

I'm so glad you enjoy your job. And it's got opportunities like this. I mean, I work hard to make sure that we can take chances like this. So that the world can be our oyster. We could explore the Met Museum. See outdoor theatre in Central Park. Fake orgasms in diners like in 'When Harry Met Sally'. This home we have is the perfect jumping off point to the rest of our adventures yet to come.

"Right, you can tell me more about this amazing UpDown Horse over dinner." And I carefully put your feet down and head into the kitchen where smells are good and veg has been free cycled from one of my client's Odd Boxes.

"How was your day?" you shout out from the sofa as I dish up. This is what we do. You tell me about your treasures and I tell you about things I've discovered too. Every day.

"Alright, I guess." I appear in our kitchenette doorway with mismatching bowls in each hand and warmth visibly rising off both in that steam of flavour that you get. I hand one to you and take the other to my end of the misshapen sofa, sitting up straight to aid digestion.

"Tools!" I hand you a spoon and fork from my pocket and produce my own from the same place.

"I was explaining today to a client about the history of massage. Some of the lesser known aspects of it."

You nod encouragingly through a mouthful, forming an 'O' with your lips at the same time, as you let some of the heat escape from burning you. It's my turn.

I spoon the sweet potato and peas around the bowl to let it cool, delaying my own first bite.

"Massage comes from all over the world. You know that right? Obviously. What with Thai massage and Swedish massage being totally different things. But it's all touch." I load up my spoon and taste the herbs that have infused the carrots that have been cooking all day. "More salt?"

"No it's good," you assure me. "Tell me about global touch." And you wiggle your fingers at me around your spoon to illustrate 'touch'.

"Right, okay. So one of the earliest 'touchers'" - I make a face at that word - "was Morgan Le Fay. You know, from the Arthurian legend. It was widely reported that she seduced Arthur to get his secrets, but in actual fact she was a masseuse. I mean, she was his sister! Euch!

"Then there was Cleopatra. Apparently - again - using seduction as a military tactic. Because that works so well and generals are clearly so led by their dicks..." I hold up a hand and stop myself. "I'm just saying, it's disrespectful to men for everyone to believe that they can be so easily led by sex hormones when they are intelligent strategic career militarists.

"Whereas if you considered that it might not have been too difficult for Cleopatra to actually just dress down and cover her head to get into the Roman encampment as a masseuse." I pop a spoonful of dinner into my mouth for added emphasis and notice that you have already devoured half of your own bowl of dinner.

"And then there's Daji. The favourite consort of King Zhou of Shang, the last king of the Shang dynasty in Ancient China. She's credited as being a classic example of how a femme fatale can bring about the downfall of a dynasty in Chinese culture. AND she was re-written as a Fox Sprite." I'm really warming up to my topic here.

"Foxy lady!" You smile at me with that dopey grin you think is so adorable.

"I'm just saying, it's not like women in any of these times had much say in the worlds they lived in and yet they're credited with the fall of civilisations with the drop of an eyelash. No, it's because 'touch'" - and here I do that thing you just did at me with my fingers to illustrate what touch is - "and seduction are always being confused. And 'touch' can tell you so much more."

You place your empty bowl on the floor next to the trainers I had so carefully tucked to the side and give me your full attention.

"Every muscle remembers where it has been." I put down my half-finished meal too. I'm not hungry anymore. "It's had to move, push, stretch throughout the day, month and year. Everywhere it's been - and crucially - everything it's reacted to and witnessed, is recorded in the knots of reaction and our personal armour of muscles. These women weren't seductresses, they were spies. Gathering information that their sources didn't even know that they were sharing. Everything a body has done and seen can be picked up - if you know how to read it properly."

I can see the penny about to drop behind your eyes.

"Some say that's where the tradition of bound feet came in, for women privy to the top of society's secrets. So that they themselves could not give away… anything."

21

And there it is. Your mouth in a perfect 'O' not for hot food, but realising intimacy has been disguising interrogation. Support has been the pretence for fact-stripping. Your feet still feel the echo of my fingers' pressure from me recent exploration. There's fire in my eyes and you can feel it.

Fire for the lumpy sofa we're sitting on that we've slept so many nights on with the promise of something different -better - soon. Somewhere better, bigger, with room for me. Promise for the extra hours I've spent touching other people so that you can lark around in the shop, that this is just transitory, before the adventure that will be the story of our lives. Of scrimping and saving, of exchanging a goddamn hand massage for food to feed us both. Led along with the dream that we were are in this together. It's tough but we've got each other and it's just for now and - you said 'no' to New York. I know. And you know I know.

Because change scares you. You were offered it - I felt it in my hands, it surprised me. But you, who has a pension and a colleague you sort of fancy but nothing has happened with yet and dinner cooked for you each night and attention - you didn't fancy it this time.

And you know how much I needed New York.

Our eyes are fixed. I pick up our bowls briskly and drop them in the kitchenette's sink, the chipped ceramic clattering dangerously.

"I'm going out." I say briskly and grab my coat off the hook on the back of the front door. "I think I might stay over with my sister."

You nod mutely.

22

And as the door closes, the latch pulls firmly behind me with a definite partition you see next to the dirty bowls, on the kitchen side - half of the German sausage neatly sliced but still remaining on the chopping board. And you gag slightly on the aftertaste of the meat you ate. And the seasoning you are now trying so hard to place.

One of Us (Jason R. Frei)

Harlan ran down the street, his shoes slapping out a quick staccato beat that matched the rhythm of his heart. He looked behind him and saw the coppers still keeping up. So far, the chase continued on for six city blocks—all over a stolen peach.

The high rises blurred past, their glass and steel construction shimmering in the sun. The day was hot and sweat dripped freely from under his black mop of hair. His dirty linen pants and t-shirt clung to his wiry frame.

Harlan had become very good at running. He did it for much of his life, either running away from something or running toward something; something he knew was just out of reach but promised to lead him to a new, grand life.

He had become an orphan at the age of six. His drug addicted mom popped one too many balloons and ended up dead in an alley. His dad gave up after that and ended up hanging from the end of a rope off the south pier. Social services picked up Harlan and he lived the next six years at St. Anne's. No one ever came for him. The nuns called him "unadoptable".

He was thin like his dad and short like his mom, so he was on the receiving end of every bad day the other kids had. They pushed him around, stole his food and generally made him do whatever they wanted. The only things that kept him out of the infirmary were his smarts and his humor. If he couldn't make the other kids laugh, he could devise a plan to get them what they wanted without anyone getting caught.

When he was ten, he found a loose corner of the fence surrounding the orphanage that could be easily pried up. He was the only one small enough and thin enough to get through it. There was a lot of free time at St. Anne's and Harlan used it to make excursions outside of the orphanage before he left completely at the age of twelve.

He came to know the city intimately. She filled his dreams and made him long for something more. She wrapped him in her warm and loving arms when he slept each night. He woke up each morning in her embrace and loved her more than he could ever say.

The first ships went off to Mars when Harlan was eight years old and just a small runt at the orphanage. The magic and mystery of it all enthralled him. He watched them come back again when he was twelve and on his own. They said Mars was inadaptable, something about the environment not being friendly to humans. Harlan knew much about that.

He slowed his pace just a bit to get the coppers closer. They needed to be almost on his heels for his disappearing trick to work. They were only a few steps behind when he turned a corner, slid behind a dumpster and wriggled his way through a hole in the wall. The coppers ran into the alley and came to a skidding halt. He lost them.

Harlan shuffled on hands and knees through a maze of cardboard boxes, wooden pallets and old rusting machines. He found this warehouse on one of his many excursions before leaving St. Anne's.

Now, this was his home. He knew every inch of the building and had made a nest deep in its core. He slipped through a matte gray plastic door and dropped into a burrow of old blankets and discarded sleeping bags. This was his den.

The den was dark and Harlan reached up and pulled a chain that lit a small light bulb. The light couldn't be seen this deep in the building, even if the coppers searched it from top to bottom. He laid back, pulled the purloined peach from his pants' pocket and took a bite. The juices ran down the sides of his smooth cheeks and pooled in the triangle indent of his neck.

When he finished, he put the pit in his pocket to dispose of later. No way was he going to leave rotting fruit in his home for ants to find. The coppers would be looking for him and he needed to lay low for a while. He packed a bag with some essentials and grabbed his modded swipe card. Time to take a teleporter to a different part of the city, to another burrow he had waiting for him.

Every large city in the world was overlaid with a system of teleportation machines. They were small one-person booths with a simple touch screen display and a card reader. All one needed to do was swipe their card and input their destination. If they had the necessary credits, a quantum gate opened, the person stepped through and they were deposited into a booth on the other side.

Shortly before Harlan escaped the orphanage, he found an unattended card at a construction site. He went directly to the library and used the card to rent some time on the web. He found a way to wire the card to give unlimited funds. He could go anywhere he wanted. He chose to go to the other side of the city. This city was the only home he knew.

He slung his bag over his shoulder and crawled through an exit tunnel to a different alleyway. He popped out without looking and almost walked right into the same two coppers he ran from earlier. They shouted when they saw him and the chase was on again.

The MagTrain terminal was packed and Harlan weaved in and out of the afternoon crowds. A smile lit up his face and his breath came easy. He ran down the steps to the underground, taking them two at a time. The underground was crammed with people going to and from work and he easily darted in and out of small bustling groups of people. He crossed the terminal, went back up another set of stairs, bee-lined to the exit and ran straight to the nearest teleporter. He ducked inside just as the coppers broke through the crowd at the exit.

Harlan swiped his card and the terminal lit up. He punched in the coordinates for his other nest and hit the big green Go button. The quantum gate opened and Harlan made to jump through, but stopped quickly. One of the wires on his swipe card had unraveled and stuck in the swiping mechanism. He tried to pull it free, but it was jammed tight. He yanked on it. The swiper shot out sparks and smoke poured out. The display crackled and wavered. Harlan gave one last tug on the wire and it snapped. He lost his balance and fell sideways through the gate. The last thing he saw was the display throwing out random numbers for his destination and then it went dark.

The concrete floor rushed up to meet Harlan as he stumbled hard out of the gate. He shivered and his limbs were cold and numb. The trip had been different, longer. He picked himself up off the floor and stamped the feeling back in his legs.

He was in a large structure, similar to the vastness of the MagTrain terminal, but empty of other people. The ceiling was high above him. Rows of plastic chairs lined up like soldiers throughout most of the room. The teleportation machine sat out in the open, not surrounded by a kiosk like the ones he was used to. A thick coating of dust rested on the floor, the chairs and the machine.

The chamber echoed with Harlan's footsteps as he walked toward an exit. At the far wall, something scurried out of the darkness. It looked similar to a rat, but with a flatter, blunter face. Smooth, red fur coated its body. Its beady, black eyes regarded Harlan warily. The rat stared for a long moment, then it snorted and scampered into a hole in the wall.

The exit led into another tunnel that angled slightly down. Doors lined the hallway every six feet or so. Harlan tried a few, but they were locked. He came to a crossroads and chose a direction at random. This hallway had no doors, but he saw a softly glowing light at the end. There was a frosted glass door set into the wall at the end of the tunnel and this one swung open on creaky hinges.

Harlan stepped through and gasped. He was in a large indoor arboretum. The domed roof gleamed dully from thick opaque glass interlaced with shiny steel girders. Leafy green trees lined the exterior of the room which contained a field of emerald colored grass. Colorful plants and flowers grew in intricate rings. A large stone fountain sat majestically in the center of the arboretum. Blue water, the color of sapphires, bubbled up from the center of the fountain, cascaded down a patterned stone pyramid and into a pool at the bottom. Harlan had only ever seen pictures like this in history books.

A stone bench faced the fountain and Harlan took a seat. He was in shock. Obviously the teleporter had malfunctioned and sent him somewhere else, but where? His city was built on the desert sands where only the hardiest vegetation survived. Water was a scarcity and deep wells were drilled to bring that water up to the city. There was no way water would be used as a centerpiece for a fountain.

Harlan thought of other lands he had seen featured in books and magazines. Much of the water on the planet had evaporated long ago due to extreme temperatures, an almost eroded ozone layer and heaps upon heaps of garbage dumped straight into the oceans. He could think of no modern city that would house an arboretum such as this. There were rumors of course, of cities lost to man. Ancient and wondrous cities that had been built for pleasure and beauty. They emphasized form over function and were like a paradise for men. Could this be one of those cities?

He decided that if this was one of those cities, then he could give in to its pleasures. He got up, stripped the grimy clothes from his body and gently eased himself into the pool. The water was warm, probably from the light filtered in through the windows. He splashed around and soaked his body in the glorious water. He floated lazily, staring up at the ceiling, picking out patterns in the steel girders.

When he felt refreshed, he went back to the bench, rummaged in his bag for some clean clothes and put them on. He walked the perimeter of the great room and found several fruit trees. He picked apples and plums and peaches and stuffed them into his bag. He bit down onto a sweet, crunchy apple and made a noise of absolute joy.

After taking his fill, he went back to the frosted glass door to begin more exploration. If there were rooms as glorious as this in the city, what else would he find?

He meandered here and there at random among the corridors. His footsteps made the only indents in the dust and he felt more and more that he had stumbled onto one of the ancient lost cities. Most of the doors he came upon were locked and he left these alone. Lost cities were usually lost for a reason and his imagination created all sorts of wild creatures and murderous ghosts lying in wait for him behind those doors. If they were locked, it was good to keep them that way.

He wandered further from the arboretum and began to see signs of wear. Cracks formed in some of the walls and the smooth stone making up the floors was chipped and rough. Red dust coated everything. He turned a corner and stopped abruptly. Harlan cupped his hand to his ear and strained to listen. He heard talking coming from down the hall, but the floor showed no signs of passage. Hesitantly, he crept forward.

The hallway ended in a large room. Wood and metal desks were arranged in neat rows. A large beige desk stood at the front of the room and a display lit up the wall behind it. A pretty blonde woman in a flower print dress moved on the screen. She read from a geography book, but the names made no sense to Harlan. Her voice sounded musical as she read off a list. A map above her head shined brightly at places as she read the names.

"Southwest Melas Basin. Holden Crater. Eberswalde Crater. Mawrth Vallis. Nili Fossae. Northeast Syrtis Major. Jezero Crater. And last, but not least"—the display lit up on a top corner and showed a red, rocky surface—"here's us, Columbia Hills, otherwise known as Gusev Crater."

Harlan felt as if he had just been punched in the stomach. The air whistled sharply through his teeth and his knees buckled. He reached out, grabbed a desk and slid into the chair. This wasn't an ancient lost city. He was on Mars!

Harlan's head reeled at the implication. Mars had been abandoned over two years earlier. All the scientists said it was inhospitable, that nothing could grow on the world. All attempts at terraforming and terramining had failed. Why had they lied? What were they running from?

A noise by the desk at the front of the room made Harlan start and he saw a red blur run under it. He got up and carefully walked down the row. Shadows pooled under the desk, but Harlan saw two beads of greenish light peering back at him. One of those rats padded forward, its whiskers twitching as it caught Harlan's scent.

31

He held out his hand and clicked his tongue. The rat clicked back and then shook its fur. A cloud of red dust emanated from the rat and when it cleared, the rat was gone. Harlan turned back toward the doorway and was startled to see two more rats watching him. They fled when they were noticed.

The classroom started to freak Harlan out and he badly wanted to find a way back to his city. His imagination took hold of his mind again and his thoughts of what lurked behind the locked doors made him shiver and shake.

He retraced his steps back toward the arboretum. This time, as he walked, he noticed smaller tracks in the dust other than his own footsteps. A feeling of dread settled over him. He imagined skitterings and scratchings behind each of the doors.

A few feet further down the hallway and he knew it was not his imagination. Small noises arose all around him. He turned and at least a dozen rats stopped in their tracks, their flinty eyes fixed on him. As Harlan watched horrified, several of the doors opened and more rats streamed out.

He turned on his heels and darted off down the hallway. The rats shrieked in chorus and gave chase. Harlan slid around corners and sprinted down the straight-aways. Rats continued flooding the hallways from opening doors. Harlan saw the frosted door of the arboretum just ahead and pushed himself faster. He reached the door, grabbed the handle and threw himself inside.

He pushed himself back up against the door and bent over, panting. His breaths came in great ragged gasps. He saw the scurrying shadows of the rats behind the door. They stopped suddenly and Harlan's blood ran cold. He slowly raised his head and looked up.

Rats filled the arboretum, a sea of writhing red fur and quivering glossy-black whiskers. A small chime sounded and the rats parted to either side. The plants and flowers shook as if a strong wind blew and then were thrust up into the air in large clods of red dirt. Silence descended over the room.

Harlan held his breath and exhaled in a strangled moan. A red-furred and muscular arm reached up out of the hole left by the plants. Its slender pink paws were tipped with sharp ivory claws. The paw gripped the emerald grass and strained as a head appeared.

The head was covered in a light red fur and two rounded pink ears jutted up from it. Grey whiskers stood out from a short, flattened nose, its nostrils two small horizontal slits. The eyes were two jet black orbs, as dark and black as a moonless night. The mouth was an upside down V that started directly under the nostrils. Small white teeth filled the mouth like sharpened grains of rice.

The creature pulled itself up out of the hole. It stood on hind legs and stretched up to a full seven feet. It was thin, lanky, its underside a darker shade of red than the rest of the body. Its tails, for there were three of them, were like wiry, pink whips. It fixed its stare on Harlan for a brief moment and then twitched its whiskers and one ear.

The other rats surrounded Harlan, crawling behind him and pushing him away from the door. Reluctantly, he approached the rat king. When he was a few feet away, the other rats stood up on their hind legs and raised their arms to the king. Harlan dropped to his knees.

The rat king walked gingerly up to Harlan and dropped down to all fours. Its nose trembled as it sniffed and snuffled at Harlan. Satisfied, it sat back on its haunches and stared into Harlan's eyes.

Harlan lost himself in the inky blackness of the rat king's eyes. The eyes were not kind, but they were also not threatening. There was an intelligence in them that dwarfed Harlan's, making him feel like the lesser creature. He instinctively knew these were the true life forms of Mars and they were the reason the scientists had fled. Harlan knew this from the gaze of the eyes, the twitching of the whiskers and the rustling of the tails. He felt a kinship to these rats and he understood them intimately, like he understood his city.

On Earth, rats were shunned and reviled, but also feared. They were ignored and kicked and trapped and killed. They were poisoned and drowned. Harlan knew all too well what it was like to be a rat. But he also knew the speed and strength of the rat, its ability to disappear in the shadows or in a hole in the wall. He also knew what he had to do next.

Harlan lay on the cool emerald grass and turned over on his back, offering his vulnerable belly to the rat king. The rat king nodded its head and put a paw on Harlan's chest. It drew a sigil into Harlan's skin with one of its pointed claws. Harlan winced, but didn't move.

The rat king sighed deeply, its breath washing over Harlan's face. It then turned and crawled back down the hole. Harlan stood and took off his backpack. He emptied its contents on the ground and opened its mouth wide. Several rats rushed forward and packed themselves inside. When he could fit no more, Harlan clasped the flap, slung it over one shoulder and left the arboretum.

He swiped his card at the teleporter and input his destination. The rest of the rats filled the great terminal hall and watched him reverently. He was their prophet, their messiah. He was the pioneer of the Martian invasion.

Danse Macabre (Dorothy Davies)

The silent figure on the gurney twitched, moved, sat up and looked around. The tag on her toe said JANE DOE which annoyed her very much. *I'm not a Jane Doe, I'm Lydia ... Lydia ...* The rest of her name escaped her, much as her memory seemed to have done.

Why am I on a gurney with a tag on my toe? Why am I cold and my veins look blue and stark and my flesh look like marble? I am NOT dead!

But – one chilled hand at her throat said otherwise. There was no pulse, no heartbeat; no warm blood rushing around a body that was beginning to sag. That annoyed her too. *My boobs never sagged! Now look...*

Look. She looked around, this dead Lydia, and saw a morgue. A cold lonely desolate morgue that held no comforts for anyone, least of all those who were delivered there on a gurney and left overnight because the staff had gone home, not bothered with yet another stiff.

She swung her legs over the side and stood up. *Well, I can still do that. Now, can I walk?*

She could. Dead Lydia staggered across the room, round the dissecting table and got to the cabinets.

I need company! She pulled and tugged and reluctantly the first drawer slid open. The man inside, elderly, lined, haggard and half starved, blinked and looked up at her.

Is it time to get up?

36

If you want.

I do. It's boring lying here like that. Nothing to look at.

I need the company.

The man sat up and pushed himself off the tray which had been holding him.

That's a good idea. Let's find some more people.

With two of them tugging at the handles, the drawers came open a good deal easier. The young girl, anorexic and pathetic, clawed at their arms as they lifted her up. *Look at me, look at me, aren't I elegant and slim and beautiful?*

The truthful answer was no, but they did not say it. *You are; you are!* She beamed and spun round, her flimsy hospital gown billowing around her. *I can dance!*

We all can but right now we want company!

Lydia pulled at another drawer with the help of the old man and the anorexic. A dark handsome youth smiled with shockingly white teeth as he sat up. *Thank you! I thought I would be stuck in there forever!* One easy movement and he got up too, swaying to an unheard rhythm. *Is it time to dance?*

Let's get everyone out first. Lydia was in charge and didn't know how she had become in charge, it had just – happened. She liked it; she had never been in charge of anything. Always the underdog, always the low paid worker following orders. Now she was issuing orders and these people were obeying her. It was a miracle and she was not about to let go of the good feelings it was generating.

I'm naked! The shock ran through her but no one had said anything, no one had ogled her, no one had touched her. *Maybe, but it isn't right!* She went back to the gurney, took up the sheet lying there, wrapped it around her body and tucked the end in securely under one arm. That felt better.

Oh, elegant, the old man observed, without a trace of sarcasm. *You wear it well, dear lady. Swan-like, I would say. What's your name?*

Lydia.

Now if I remember my Greek mythology, there was a swan that went to Leda, which is close enough to your name, dear lady. I want to change that. You are a swan, wrapped in white as you are, as elegant as you are and as thoughtful as you are. Let's call you Leda instead of Lydia. It sounds so much more romantic.

Leda. Lydia. She turned the names over in her mind. *Leda will do fine*, she said eventually, with a big smile. *Thank you. No one has ever said anything that nice to me in my whole life.*

Well, they should have done. I mean, there you are, you had every chance to walk right out the door and leave, instead you opened drawers and let us out.

Well, it was because I wanted company, she confessed, rather than take credit for something that was not right.

He shook his head. *Maybe, maybe, but you had your chance and you chose to stay. Now, let's get everyone else out, shall we?*

Combined effort, they all worked at opening the drawers, releasing a white cheeked old lady with sharply knowing eyes and a loving smile, a middle-

38

aged man still looking for his pens and papers, the reason for his existence, the little girl who had collided with a bus or a bus had collided with her, either way she was not pretty any more but no one said a word, they took her hands and they all danced round the dissecting table and laughed a great hollow laugh that no one could hear but them.

The dark man told them jokes at which they all roared with laughter, the old lady told them of her children which brought tears to their eyes, the old man spoke of sunny days on a river bank fishing with grandchildren and some of them grew nostalgic. Then they danced again to refresh their senses and their spirits and their energies and told one another this was the best night they had ever had in their entire existence.

Dawn touched the sky with pink fingers. One by one, without saying a word why they were doing it, they climbed back into their drawers and one by one Leda, still in her white robe which made her look like a swan, closed the drawers with a supreme effort.

When they were all sleeping again, she gracefully performed a solitary dance around the room, remembering the feel of rhythm making the feet move, the thrill of a tune running through the head, the sway of arms and hands. Then she grew tired, it had been a long night and an exhausting one, but oh what fun she had experienced!

She climbed back onto the gurney, laid the sheet out and stared up at the ceiling, remembering how it felt to dance.

Just before she fell asleep forever, she wondered what the mortuary attendant would think when he found her tag on the floor…

Legion (Jason R. Frei)

Cymun's eyes fluttered open as the lights in his cabin flashed and a klaxon sounded. He unplugged himself from the charging station and strode to the vid-comm.

"Cymun to the bridge. Status report."

"Captain Volshenko reporting." The voice was a deep baritone with a thick Bulgarian accent. "We have answered a level three distress call. Look out your window and then report to the bridge."

Cymun signed off and set the translucency of his wall to zero. The wall seemingly vanished as Cymun looked out at the expanse of space. A mining vessel drifted listlessly a few meters to starboard. Rust stained its hull, but otherwise it looked intact. Cymun knew first-hand that looks could be deceiving. He dialed the wall back up and made his way to the bridge.

The Argo was a star-class exploration vessel. Her mission was to travel within the five known galaxies and assist in setting up new bases on the outer rim. These bases would be the forefront of new exploration to the unknown galaxies. Cymun was newly assigned to the Argo as a liaison for the Commonwealth. He had not made a great impression with the crew so far. His arrival on the bridge was met with resentment and derision.

"Nice of you to finally join us," said Volshenko.

Cymun took his seat next to the Captain. The derelict mining vessel took up the whole of the viewscreen. "What do we know so far, Captain?"

The Captain stared straight ahead and waved at the screen. "The Daedalus, a mining dreadnought from the Sirius system. It wasn't due in this sector for at least two months. We're not even sure if it made it to the mining colony."

"Have you hailed the ship?" asked Cymun.

Volshenko's face turned a dark shade of red and his brows furrowed into a deep V. He turned slowly to Cymun. "Are you questioning my leadership, ambassador?"

Cymun's face remained passive. "Of course not, Captain. I am just making sure we are operating according to protocol."

Volshenko kept his voice even, but could not hide his anger. "Everything on my ship operates according to protocol. You can report that back to your superiors."

Cymun started to reply, but Volshenko cut him off with a look of pure malice. Cymun was an uninvited guest and he knew better to keep quiet so his observations could occur without interruption. He nodded his head slightly to the Captain.

Volshenko turned and addressed his first officer. "Get a landing party ready, Commander. Take him"—Volshenko thrust his thumb at Cymun—"with you."

"Yes sir," said Commander Lamere who turned to Cymun. "Get your stuff ready and meet at the boarding hatch. You have five minutes or we leave without you. Understood?"

Cymun nodded and gave a small salute. He returned to his room to pack his bag. Maybe this was his chance to show the crew how useful he could be.

***

The landing party had already started their trek across the boarding tunnel when Cymun got there. Lamere stood waiting impatiently and ushered him into the tunnel without a word.

Cymun emerged on the other side. Three armored Marines stood at the front of the party with bright lights shining from the muzzles of their heavy rifles. Geo-engineer Wen and Tach Sergeant Mitchell rounded out the party.

Lamere took the lead and guided them to the bridge. The corridors were empty of crew. No evidence of any struggle could be found. The bridge doors were fused shut, as if welded from the inside. Mitchell accessed an external comm station.

"The distress signal isn't coming from the bridge," said Mitchell. Confusion and concern coated his high voice. "It's from the science lab."

Mitchell called up a diagnostic program that displayed a blueprint of the ship's schematics. Lamere coordinated with Wen and one of the Marines.

"I want both of you to go to the lab," he said. He called up a routine that mapped the quickest route and scanned it to the Marine's wrist communicator.

"The rest of you will come with me," said Lamere. "We'll take this route"- he indicated it with his finger-"and head to engineering. There's a service tunnel that should take us directly underneath the bridge."

***

Wen and Kline, the Marine assigned to her, made their way to the science lab without issue. The door had been mag-locked from the inside, so Kline used a cutting torch to disable the lock and gain entry.

Wen stepped through and immediately stopped, a long whistle trilled from her sharp avian mouth. In the center of the lab was a large upright stone. It was mottled red and black. Light pulsed dimly from its center. A naked figure lay at the base of the stone. The body was sexless and hairless. One pale arm was outstretched, its hand clenched so tightly to the rock that it appeared to be merged with it.

Wen briefly examined the body and then dismissed it. She marveled at the rock and set about taking readings and photos from her portable DAT-kit. Kline wandered the room, looking for any indications of what happened.

Wen checked the readouts. The stone's composition was completely unknown to her. It gave off a low but steady heat signal with no radiation. She pulled out a micro laser drill, cutting into the rock to take a few samples.

She abruptly turned, her head cocked, listening.

"What is it?" asked Kline. His grip on the rifle tightened and swung into a ready position.

"Don't you hear it?" Wen closed her eyes, her head titled up to the rock. "It sounds like whispering."

Kline raised the comm volume on his helmet, but heard nothing. Wen swayed back and forth, murmuring incomprehensively to herself. Kline approached. He reached out to grip her arm.

Without warning, the pale, nude body on the floor darted out its free arm and clutched at the Marine's leg. Kline yelped in surprise. He swung the butt end of the rifle down onto the figure's arm. The arm snapped, but its hand dug deep into Kline's leg. He hopped around and slammed the rifle down again, this time aiming for the head.

The butt cracked sharply against the attacker's skull. Viscous black fluid spurted out. The body jerked rigid, as if an electric current ran through it and Kline's body spasmed. He dropped his rifle and screamed, his mouth opening impossibly wide.

His eyes darkened to an inky black and receded into his skull, leaving small dark pits where they used to be. He stopped screaming and turned toward Wen.

Wen muttered and swayed as all of this transpired, oblivious to the carnage around her, transfixed only on the stone. Kline grabbed her by the head, pressing his thumbs into her eyes. Wen's body shuddered and her mouth extended open. An inhuman howling issued from it. Her body shook fitfully. When her shaking subsided, she joined the other two. Black ooze trickled from the pits where her eyes once were. The trio walked in unison out of the lab.

***

Lamere swiped the mag-lock for engineering and the door whooshed open. The emergency lights gave the room an eerie aspect. Mitchell went to the control console and punched the reset switch. Nothing happened. He tried again with the same result.

"Power's out, Commander."

"Can you reroute from non-essential sectors?" asked Lamere.

Mitchell pulled a hatch open from under the console and got to work. Cymun walked to the reactor core and peered inside its window. A dark mass restricted his view.

Mitchell shouted in triumph as the lights kicked on. The engine hummed to life. Cymun barked a yelp of surprise, stepped back and fell over a conduit hose.

Lamere laughed and then stopped abruptly. His face blanched as he looked through the reactor bay window. The charred remains of a body were pressed against the window from inside the chamber. Its flesh was still pink where it fused to the glass. One eye was open and looked glassily at them. Mitchell wretched and threw up behind the console he was working on.

"My God," whispered Lamere. "What the hell happened here?"

"Commander," said Lewis, the shorter of the two Marines. "We've lost contact with the other team."

"What do you mean 'lost contact'?" asked Lamere.

"We've tried radioing them several times and they aren't answering, sir," said Lewis.

Gibson, the other Marine chimed in. "There's also some localized comm disruption, sir. We're not able to get a signal out to the Argo."

"Dammit," shouted Lamere. He pointed at the Marines. "Both of you come with me to engineering." He turned to Cymun. "You take Mitchell and get to the bridge. Once there, establish a connection with the Argo and wait for me."

Cymun nodded as Lamere stomped off with the two Marines. Mitchell wiped his mouth on the back of the sleeve and then popped open the hatch to a support tunnel. He waved his arm in a flourish. "After you."

***

Lamere and the Marines trod carefully to engineering. The corridor lights flickered on and off throwing ominous shadows across the walls. Their footfalls echoed back and forth in the empty corridors. The Marines stayed at high alert sweeping the hallways from side to side with their rifles.

They came to an intersection not far from engineering when Gibson halted. He raised his fist for the others to stop.

"What is it?" asked Lamere.

Gibson shook his head as a gesture for silence. He then made several hand signals to Lewis who crept silently forward to the T at the end of the hallway. Gibson backed him up by staying several paces behind and to the right.

Lewis was a few feet from the intersection when the door to his right burst open and the animated body of Wen collided with him. His rifle sent off a burst of bullets that tore through Wen and drove her against the wall. Instead of slumping to the floor, she bounced off and latched onto Lewis.

Gibson ran up with his rifle poised to deliver a blow when Kline stepped out of the open door. Gibson slid to a halt, brought up his gun and fired a burst at Kline. Half of Kline's head ruptured into a black splatter, but the body spun around and clutched at Gibson.

Lewis and Gibson wrestled with their attackers, while Lamere turned and fled. He looked back as he ran and crashed hard into a third body. The nude body grappled him to the ground and gripped his neck like an iron vise. Lamere's body convulsed just once before his neck snapped. As if on cue, Lamere, Gibson and Lewis shrieked in unison and then rose anew.

***

Cymun and Mitchell climbed out of the hatch and into the bridge. A chalky mist hung in the air. The stench of charred flesh assailed them. The only thing piercing the haze was the flashing of the emergency lights.

Mitchell coughed and hacked at the smell. Cymun made his way blindly to the central command console. He felt around the console until he found the button he wanted and pressed it. The fog cleared out rapidly as a fan spun overhead. Mitchell made a small, strangled sound.

The bridge looked like a charnel house. Splashes of red and black splattered the instrument panels like an impressionist painting. Bodies, both clothed and naked, tangled together in the room. The smell came from the bodies. They were scorched and in varying states of decay. Some were charred to the point of carbonization while others appeared melted with bits of flesh, hair and cloth poking out from the gory mess. The consoles themselves were blackened and damaged. It looked like a fire storm ravaged the bridge.

Cymun walked over to Mitchell and helped him to his feet. Cymun nodded reassuringly. "Come on. Let's see what we can get working."

***

Cymun and Mitchell got rudimentary power running to the bridge. The main viewscreen showed the Argo coupled to the Daedalus, oblivious as to what was going on inside. They scavenged the salvageable parts and stitched together a communications array like a Frankenstein's monster. They couldn't send a direct communication to the Argo, but they figured out how to send different signal patterns. They were in the midst of modifying a distress signal when a pounding started on the bridge door.

"Are any of the hall cams active?" asked Cymun.

Mitchell ran to the vid console and started punching buttons. "The main viewscreen controls are fried, but I can probably route some video to the Captain's chair."

"Do it."

Mitchell popped open a port on the console and fished the wiring out. He cut and spliced several of the wires and then fed them under the board into different ports. He flipped a switch. Sparks flew, but the power held. A tinny sound issued from the Captain's chair. Both Mitchell and Cymun ran to the chair.

The screen was about the size of Cymun's hand and right now only static played on it. Mitchell bent down and smacked the side of the armrest. The screen came into focus.

There were three individuals outside the bridge slamming their fists against the steel door. Small dents appeared and the door bent slightly inward.

Mitchell squinted at the screen. "Aren't those the Marines that came with us?"

A noise from behind startled both Cymun and Mitchell. They turned as a head appeared from the support hatch in the floor. Half of the head was missing and black muck dripped from the chin.

Mitchell grabbed a span wrench from the nearest console and ran over to the hatch. He swung the wrench in a downwards arc and hit the creature full in what was left of the face. Its head snapped back and it slid down the ladder. Mitchell slammed the hatch shut, then locked it with an emergency override.

"What the hell was that?" His scream had an unhinged edge to it.

The pounding on the door became louder. The seam where the doors met was open enough for Cymun to see the figures on the other side. A pale arm reached through the door. Its fist was pulped and dripped a thick black fluid on the floor.

Cymun turned toward Mitchell and shouted, but his warning was not quick enough. The door to the Captain's quarters opened silently and Wen rushed out. Her torso was riddled with seeping bullet holes. She tackled Mitchell and they crashed into a console. Wen fell on top of Mitchell and she pounded on him with impossibly strong hands. A shudder went through his body as he shrieked. He rolled to his side and stood up. Mitchell and Wen faced Cymun together.

Cymun turned to put space between him and the monstrosities as the bridge doors flung open. Two of the Marines darted in pinning Cymun to a wall. He struggled but could not break free from their iron grasp. Cymun calmed himself down to conserve his energy. He looked into the blackened pits of the nearest Marine's eyes.

"What is going on here?" he asked.

Mitchell walked up behind the Marines and addressed Cymun.

"We are Legion." The voice echoed and reverberated around the room as it came not just from Mitchell, but from all the others in the room as well.

"Long ago, we traveled to your world to conquer it. During our crusade, we were met by one of your holy armies. We fought their champion and we lost. As punishment, he banished us to the outer edges of space. We found a living star in the confines of space and possessed it. We have traveled the expanses of the universe in order to finish our conquest.

51

"The journey has been long and the star we once inhabited grew smaller and smaller. Fate was with us. One of your own starships found us and brought us on board. They fought us and we were almost destroyed, but now Fate has brought you to us. You will take us the rest of the way."

Mitchell pushed the Marines aside, reached out his hand and pressed it firmly to Cymun's chest. A look of confusion passed over Mitchell's face. Wen and the three Marines let out a gasp of disbelief. Mitchell took Cymun's head in both hands. He squeezed, but there was resistance.

Cymun smiled. He raised his hands and peeled Mitchell's from his head. Mitchell struggled, but could not keep his grip.

"What is this?" cried Mitchell and the others in unison.

Cymun pushed Mitchell back and made room for himself. "As you said, you possess the living; however, I am not alive. I am an advanced artificial intelligence housed in a cybernetic-enhanced body. I look, feel and respond like a living being, but I am so much more."

Mitchell stepped back as the three Marines moved in. Cymun ducked into a crouch and leapt over the lot of them into the middle of the room. He flipped the switch on the makeshift communications array hoping that the Argo would receive the signal and react.

Hands grabbed him from behind. He whipped his head back and felt the satisfying crunch of a nose. He felt the gore of the broken face splatter his neck. He grabbed the hands, flipping the body over himself.

Two others tried to grab him, but Cymun was faster and stronger. He thrust both arms out and hit the incoming bodies in the chest, driving them backward. Cymun spun around and darted to the Captain's chair. Mitchell dove for his legs, but Cymun delivered a vicious kick that sent Mitchell rolling.

Cymun tore open the command panel on the Captain's chair and input a series of numbers. The lights switched to red as a klaxon sounded. A soothing voice spoke over the loudspeaker.

"The ship's self-destruct has been activated. You have one minute to evacuate."

Cymun felt the ship lurch slightly and heard the thunk of the boarding tunnel being retracted. Cymun watched as the Argo left the side of the Daedalus and cruised out of the blast zone.

Cymun sat down in the Captain's chair as the loudspeaker counted down to zero. The possessed bodies pressed in on him. Cymun smiled, knowing that he just saved the world.

***

Captain Volshenko received the modified distress signal mere moments after Cymun activated it and the self-destruct. He quickly thumbed the communications stud.

"Captain to boarding hatch. Disengage tunnel immediately!" His voice was high and pitched.

"Negative, Captain," replied a crewman. "We have a man in the tunnel."

"Get him out of there now!" bellowed the Captain. "The Daedalus is set to self-destruct!"

The crewman opened the hatch door and yelled to the man crossing. "Commander Lamere! Get on board now!"

Lamere sprinted through the hatch and fell to the floor. Another crewman threw a blanket over the Commander's body and dragged him the rest of the way in. The other team members disengaged the tunnel and gave the all clear.

Lamere was helped to a bench and a slew of questions were directed at him. No one noticed the blackened eyes or the shard of dark rock gripped in his hand until it was too late.

Victims of War (Dorothy Davies)

Trains are more important now than ever, now that we are at war. Have you not seen them, the young men in khaki, hiding their fears behind gallows humour and stiff upper lip, when you know well they are not old enough to leave home, to face the guns, the foe in all their fierceness to push us out of Europe...

My problem is simple. I have a form of second sight. I see the men; I see the light around them. I can tell before they go who will come back missing a limb or even two, for those limbs have no light around them. I could go to them and say, 'don't go, don't go, for you will come home legless, armless or wounded in some terrible way.' But they would laugh at me and get on the train anyway. I am no more than a foolish porter.

But the real nightmare I live with day after day are the ones I see with no heads, just a skull Oh yes, I see the ones who will not return and how sad, how heart-breaking sad is it to see them for are they not young and energetic and have much to give to this world?

How many are so shown to me? I cannot say. In a crowd there could be 3 or 4 of them, maybe more. I see the skulls; I turn away for I cannot bear the thought of the loss of the young men.

The draining of the country is how I see it. Those who would work, those who would labour, those who would teach, those who would lead, they are heading for the Front, that mystical ever moving

55

ever dangerous and treacherous Front, where they will come face to face with the enemy, with gunfire, with barbed wire and with every fear there is known to man.

They will come home damaged in body and in mind.

So you see me, a porter here on this station, ushering the young men onto the trains, smart in their uniforms, casual in their humour, dying inside with fear and gut wrenching longing not to be there, they are busy with their mask of indifference to their fate and I am someone they ignore completely. I wave my green flag, I blow my whistle; I send the train out of the station to the coast where they will board the ships that will take them into Hell and damnation. For they will return changed beyond belief, beyond recognition, except for those who wear the skulls, those who will end up under grass in a foreign land.

Those who boarded those trains are the lucky ones. Those who stayed behind suffered the agonies of being left behind.

I wanted to go. I thought I had to go.

But I looked in the mirror the day I was due to go to the recruiting office, I looked and I saw –

A skull.

And I could not go.

I stay here, with my cowardice. In my own hell.

Together in the End (Travis Mushanski)

Hannah weaved past the teenagers jostling into each other on the running path and proceeded to climb a small man-made hill overlooking the city curated park. She stood with her arms on her waist, sucking in large gasps of air. Her lungs burned from the strain of the run, but she smiled through the pain. She glanced down at her watch to see her time was slightly better than the day before.

She drank from her water bottle and admired the park from her viewpoint. Her timing had been nearly perfect today: she caught the sun just before it sank behind the horizon, brushing the sky with beautiful shades of pink, orange and yellow. The park lamps began popping on throughout the park, sending cascading lamplight across the glassy surface of the man-made lake at the park's center.

She casually walked down the hill to slow her heart rate for the second half of her run. During her teenage years, she had been active on her high school track team, mostly long-distance running, but quickly lost interest while working through college. Life, as it has the tendency to do, whipped by Hannah in a whirlwind. Before she knew it, she was married to the love of her life and pregnant with her first child.

Hannah's first urge to take up running again came during one of her child's mid-afternoon naps. She had another nine months of maternity remaining before she had to return to work and the long days at home with her daughter made her restless. She craved the outside world. More than anything, she missed the single-mindedness that running brought.

She smiled thinking about her first evening run, nearly a month ago to the day, when she couldn't make it to the place she now stood. In the yellow light of a park lamp, she adjusted her Spotify playlist on her Apple watch. She wanted something upbeat and fun from her teenage years. No Doubt blasted through her earbuds, flooding her system with nostalgia and endorphins.

There was a light pinch at her elbow; she gasped and swung around in surprise. A man with dark hair held his hand out, saying something she couldn't hear over the streaming music. He gritted his crooked teeth and mimed something with his ears.

Hannah breathed a sigh of relief and shook her head in embarrassment. "I'm so sorry," she began while removing the ear buds. "You surprised me."

"I was just wondering what you were listening to." The man chuckled, pointing to her ears. He grasped his hands behind his back and flashed her a smile: wrinkle lines creased his forehead, revealing him to be older than Hannah first thought.

Hannah scrunched her face and tilted her head. The stranger remained quiet while waiting for a response. She tilted her Apple watch to the man and said, "Just some No Doubt. An old band from the—"

"What's your name?" He cut Hannah off mid-sentence. He gestured to himself and said, "Cyril."

Hannah grinned and glanced around herself at the pitch-black park, lit only by a handful of lamps.

"Listen, Cyril. I'm flattered. I really am, but I'm married." She flashed her wedding ring and back stepped away from the man. *God forbid a woman can go for a run without a man having to 'take his shot'.*

"Well, the least you could do is tell me your name?" Cyril sounded crestfallen, his physical stature drooped.

"Have a nice evening, Cyril," Hannah said with a smile. She turned to jog away, but an iron grip seized her elbow. She looked back to see Cyril's wide frantic eyes; a straight razor glimmered between his sausage fingers.

"Now, sweetheart," his voice was harsh and full of broken glass. "Let's say the two of us have a little fun. I've gone and introduced myself and I think it's mighty rude that you isn't telling me your—"

Hannah pulled away from Cyril and, when he yanked her back towards him, she used the momentum to drive her knee into his groin. He doubled over with a guttural groan and the razor skipped across the paved walkway.

Hannah bolted from the creep writhing in pain. From somewhere behind her, she heard him growl, "You fucking bitch!" She chanced a quick glance back and was shocked to see he was already on his feet, shambling towards her with the razor in hand.

She ran as hard and as fast she could, but it was only a matter of time before her body betrayed her. Her quads already ached and her chest started to constrict from exhaustion. Each time she looked back, the crazed man was closer.

Facebook! The word shot off a flare of hope in her mind. *I can use the app to call for help.* She frantically swiped through the plethora of icons populating her home screen. Her gaze repeatedly swept back and forth between the watch, the forest and the madman. At some point she realised her feet had moved onto the plush grass of the park, but she pushed forward, weaving through trees while the world grew dark. Hannah slowed to a jog and the world suddenly turned bleak. She stared at the words scrawled across her watch in bewilderment: no service.

She came to a full stop and looked up from her watch to see Cyril standing ten feet in front of her. Nothing but forest surrounded them now, the walking path and lamps were a distant memory. Moonlight trickled through the forest canopy to highlight his wide eyes and snarling mouth. The Apple watch trembled on her wrist, casting a faint aura around Hannah's horrified face.

Cyril wheezed. Sweat seeped out of his every pore. His greasy laugh echoed through the trees. "Bad girls need to be punished," he grumbled. Each word filtered through labored breathing. "Now come to Papa and we can end this farce."

Cyril took a step towards Hannah, but a rustling sound made him stop. He managed to spit out a confused grunt before a shadowed fist cracked him in the teeth. He collapsed into a group of bushes, out cold.

"Come on, let's get out of here before he gets back up," the shadowed figure called out to Hannah. He moved into the pale moonlight and held out his hand for her to take. He breathed heavy, sweat trickling down his temples.

Hannah studied the man before taking his outstretched hand. He reminded her of a boy she dated once in college: short brown hair, bright blue eyes and dimpled cheeks. There was a strange sensation of homesickness that made her trust this stranger.

"Chad," the man said. He gripped her hand and they scrambled through the darkness. Hannah had become disorientated during the chase, but with Chad's guidance, they quickly approached the distant lamplight.

"I'm Hannah," she responded, realizing she no longer held her water bottle. Her throat was dry and scratchy.

"My car is parked nearby," he explained. "You close? Or should I drive you over to your own vehicle?"

They breached the lamplight highlighting the park path; they felt like they just finished a marathon. Hannah gripped her sides, trying to catch her breath. She looked around and realized she was on the wrong side of the park. "Shit. Shit. Shit. Shit," she cursed, fighting back tears.

"You, okay? Did he hurt you?" Chad asked, staring into her eyes.

"No. I'm fine. Well, not fine," she stumbled on her words, "but not hurt."

"Ok, good. Listen, Hannah," he gripped her shoulders to calm her. "I'm parked just on the other side of those bushes, alright?" Hannah replied with a silent nod. She wiped sweat and tears out of her eyes.

Chad held the door open and helped Hannah into the passenger seat of the Ford Escape. She smiled and sunk into the vehicle's plush interior. She sighed a breath of relief.

A bright light sparked to life in Chad's pocket and Hannah watched him fish out a cellphone. He squinted at the screen and made a worried expression. He glanced at Hannah through the Escape's windshield and started to frantically type a text message.

"I can just walk from here if you want," Hannah suggested when Chad climbed into the driver's seat. "If you need to be somewhere, or whatever."

"No worries, Hannah." He flashed her a smile. "I'll have you home in no time." The engine rumbled to life, and Chad accelerated into the deserted street.

"Home?" Butterflies fluttered through her stomach. "You mean to my car, right?"

"Oh, ya. That's what I meant, babe."

Babe? She squinted at Chad, analysing his features in the dull street lights. "I'm pretty sure my car was the other way." She coiled against the passenger-side door.

Chad remained silent; Eyes wide, never blinking. The shadows in the Escape twisted and obscured his features. A silence ate its way through the vehicle: all that remained were Hannah's twitching heart and Chad's raspy breathing.

"Here is good." Hannah's trembling voice cut through the silence. "You can just let me out here," she chuckled nervously.

"Oh, shit. Ya, sorry, Hannah." His voice was light hearted and charismatic, but his physical demeanor didn't change. He eased the vehicle over to the curb.

"Thanks for the help, Chad." She twisted her lips into a half smile and pushed against her door. No matter how much force she exerted on the door, it did not move.

"Child safety locks," Chad said in a monotone voice.

Hannah's shoulders dipped, and she turned to face Chad. She was ready for a fight, but so was he: there was a pistol aimed at her chest. Hannah was about to scream when the back door swung open and the car rocked from the added weight.

"Why'd ya have to hit me so hard, man?"

That voice! No, it couldn't be, Hannah thought. She glanced over her shoulder to see Cyril rubbing his bruised jaw.

Hannah screamed and threw herself at her passenger side door. Her fists pounded the glass window until her knuckles split, smearing blood across the glass.

Chad sighed and slammed the butt of his gun into Hannah's temple.

The milky cataracts faded from Chad's eyes and his chin slumped to his chest. A haze of anesthesia drifted around his head, making it difficult to regain consciousness. He tried to move, but his arms and legs were bound with rope to a wooden chair.

Chad looked up into a blurry visage of death. It appeared to be clawing its way into our reality with strange spasmodic movements. He clamped his eyes shut and recoiled against the chair. All that remained was a miasma of musty decay.

"No," a crackled, feminine voice cried out. "You must see." An icy hand gripped his forehead and drew open his eyelids. A second hand hovered in front of his face, gripping a straight razor between grey fingers.

"Who are you? Where am I?" Chad gulped.

"You were telling me about Hannah Wilson," the raspy voice explained. The foul stench of rotting flesh wafted out from the shadows of the figure's hood.

"I don't know anyone by that name," Chad wined. He stared wide-eyed at his own reflection in the straight razor's polished surface.

"You can't lie to us, Chad." The hooded figure released its grip on his forehead. "Was it by your hand that her throat was slashed?" It tilted its head back to reveal a slashed throat, gaping open with rotten flesh. A delicate hand traced the blackened wound; a mischievous grin formed above trails of corrupting decay.

"It was Cyril," Chad blurted out. He squirmed against his binding. "He killed the woman. I just—"

"You just served her up to for the real monster to feast upon?" The figure's harsh voice cut him off. It drew back its hood to reveal the gaunt death mask of Hannah Wilson.

"No. No, it's impossible," Chad panicked and squirmed to get away from the dead woman. "We—"

Anger flared in Hannah's lifeless eyes. "Beat me? Raped me? Slit my throat and left me for

64

dead?" She pressed the razor into Chad's jugular, careful to not break skin. She leaned in and whispered into his ear, "Sound right, *babe*?"

"It's true. It's all true," Chad cried. Tears flowed down his cheeks. His entire body quivered from fear and desperation. A puddle formed beneath his chair, and the sharp stench of piss filled the room.

"What a pathetic piece of shit you are," Hannah said with distain.

"I'm sorry," he called out through the tears. "I don't wanna die. It was Cyril. Take him! I'll do anything you want," Chad begged.

Hannah shook her head back and forth in disbelief. "You took me away from my new-born daughter and the man I loved. You destroyed my family," she said quietly in her raspy voice, making sure to annunciate each word. "And you want me to show you mercy?"

Hannah's body shook with a low ghastly laughter that filled their confined room. She stumbled to the floor in a mad fit of laughter. Tears of blood flowed down her face as the laughter steadily grew maniacal. The room reverberated madness until it evolved into screams of terror.

Hannah drove the razor into Chad's side and the cacophony instantly silenced. A wide smile formed beneath the rivers of crimson coating her face. Chad's silent scream of pain cascaded through her reanimated corpse with fiery bliss.

"Fucking, bitch," Chad growled, rabid ferocity filled his features. Blood quickly soaked through his shirt.

"There's the feral dog we promised to neuter," she licked coagulated blood from her lips. "I knew you were in there."

"Fuck you mean, 'we'?"

Hannah held a finger to her lips and tussled his sweaty hair. He tried to bite her hand but she giggled and walked past him. She exited the cell via a metal door that clamored shut behind her.

The moment the rear door closed, the door in front of Chad squealed open on rusty hinges. Another robed figure glided into the cinderblock room bearing the same putrescent aroma as Hannah. It froze before Chad, grasping a corkscrew against its chest in a loving embrace.

"Hey, Chad. Remember me?"

Chad watched the door close behind the figure and for the briefest moment, he saw beyond its threshold into the horrors beyond. Dozens of robed figures stood in absolute silence, patiently waiting for their turn to confront their murderer. Each gripped a weapon saturated with their pain and suffering.

Not even the sealed cell door could suppress Chad's screams. They broke free of the sound-proof room and rippled across the endless void.

Fungus Among Us (Jason R. Frei)

The skies opened up on the second afternoon of our hike. Great fat drops of rain fell like meteors cutting through the forest, drenching us to the bone. Neither Paul nor I expected a storm this early in the season. The air still carried a chill and the barren trees allowed the rain full access to us.

The storm continued for the rest of the afternoon. It collected in small streams that ran in rivulets down the trail. We slogged uphill through the mud and finally crested the top as darkness descended. The flat, rutted trail lay before us. Water pooled in pockets. We found it difficult to find a spot to set up camp for the night. I wanted to continue until we found something reasonably dry, but Paul, ever the more practical of the two of us, insisted we go off trail and find a high spot as the rain made no sign of stopping.

By the time we found a dry and elevated spot, midnight was nearly upon us. We set up camp on a hillock surrounded by evergreen trees. The water level rose significantly. I set up the tents as Paul created a fire from the least wet pieces of wood he found. The rain stopped as I hammered in the last tent peg. It had conspired against us all day and, finding us done for the night, it too chose to rest.

Paul got a nice fire going to dry us off. I worked on cooking a hearty stew. We were both in good spirits despite how miserable the day had been. The clouds scattered and stars dotted the night sky. The still water reflected the light from the stars like tiny floating mirrors.

We gathered more wood for the fire as the stew thickened. The west side of our campsite butted up against a line of the evergreens. The cones had already ripened and fallen to the forest floor. Odd mushrooms—bone dry and white—sprouted out of the trunks about a foot from the ground. I brushed up against a clump when I reached down for a fallen branch. The mushrooms disintegrated into a fine powder and got carried away by a slight breeze. Some of the dust got in my mouth. It tasted rancid, like rotten meat.

I headed back to the camp with an armful of kindling and noticed other mushrooms at the edges of the rain ponds. They grew smaller and rounder with a sickly green color. They smelled musty, like a college dorm during Spring break.

I mentioned the mushrooms to Paul and he saw them too. It was peculiar that we saw none during our hike the past day and a half. Paul stated they must be a variety that only sprouts in the presence of large quantities of water, but it was rare for any mushroom varieties to crop up this quick.

I shivered and it wasn't just from the cold. We changed the topic, talking about the wonderful sights we had seen. We ate our stew and soon forgot about the mushrooms. After dinner, we smoked cigars and I opened a bottle of small batch bourbon. We leaned back, watched the stars and enjoyed each other's company. It was shortly after that we retired to our tents.

I awoke abruptly, half sobbing and gasping for air. The sharp edges of a disturbing dream slid from my brain.

I remembered floating on the water with the stars all around me. I bobbed up and down on the calm, serene water in a hypnotic rhythm. The waters slowly picked up speed, spinning me in a vortex. I thrashed as hands pulled me down into the murky depths. The water crashed over me filling my mouth with the taste of rot and decay. The last thing I remembered before waking up was the green cap of a mushroom thrusting up through my throat and out of my mouth.

I slipped quietly out of my tent. The gibbous moon hung low over the horizon providing the only light. By now the fire was nothing more than embers. The half empty bottle of bourbon lay off to the side of the firepit. I walked briskly to it and downed three swallows straight from the bottle. A small dribble ran down my chin. I wiped it off on my nightshirt and felt something clammy on my neck. I scratched at the spot and a small white mushroom cap came away in my hand.

My mind snapped back to my dream. I thrashed around, finding more mushrooms clinging to my garments. I rolled on the moist ground, crushing what I could not reach with my hands. I ran to Paul's tent and thrust open the flap. What I saw inside almost snapped my mind.

Paul lay completely still on his back. Mushrooms of all shapes, sizes and colors covered him. Thick golden chanterelles encased his feet. Brown morels jutted up from his shins and thighs like a colony of corral. Clusters of enoki, their long white stems and small caps swaying slightly, dotted his stomach and spread out among the chanterelles and morels. Oyster mushrooms, like surreal Dali-esque table tops, grew rampantly on his arms and sides. Black truffles covered Paul's neck and cheeks giving him the appearance of a beard. Great red and green toadstools jutted up from his chest like tombstones in a graveyard. Only the top half of Paul's head remained free from this nightmare.

I started to reach in to tear the mushrooms from his body when I heard a disturbing noise from behind me. I ran to a stack of piled wood and hunkered down behind it.

The water at the far edge of our encampment roiled and frothed. Large milky white bubbles broke the surface popping over and over again. Small grotesque creatures emerged from the water. They seemed human shaped, but bore more of a resemblance to a gastropod. Slime slicked their greying skin. Their bodies bore no visible joints. Black lidless eyes stuck up from antennae. Their heads rested directly on their bodies with no necks. A round black shrivelled hole in the middle of the face passed for a mouth. The fetid smell of swamp assaulted my nose.

The creatures oozed onto the land and glided through the mud. They measured half a dozen and converged on the center of the camp. They went first to the tents. Two of them rummaged through my tent, but finding it empty, joined the others at Paul's tent. They removed Paul and put him on the backs of two of them. The creatures then wriggled to the end of the campsite and entered the woods where I first encountered the mushrooms.

I followed at a distance so as not to be discovered. Once under the cover of the pines, the creatures left a mucous trail over the soft needles. This made maintaining my distance easier. The darkness thickened under the dense trees. I almost didn't see the clearing until I was right at its edge.

A thin mist hung over the glade shrouding it in mystery. The stars winked in the sky above, but their light was not bright enough to penetrate the gloom of the opening before me. Hesitantly, I moved forward.

The wet ground sucked at my feet as I walked. Bulrushes poked up from the mist like pikes on a battlefield. A soft wind blew and the heads of the bulrushes hit each other, making muted thumps. Peepers and bullfrogs sung a discordant song—the high pitched sleigh bell of the peepers and the deep resonant bass of the bullfrogs. They mixed with the muffled bulrushes and the squelching of the mud. causing me to feel apprehensive.

A form took shape in the murkiness. As I got closer, a cave opened up in front of me. Giant slabs of fungi outlined the mouth of the cave. White mossy mold spread across the roof and waved in the wind. The odor of swamp drifted out lazily. I heard indescribable noises and a soft light glowed from deep inside. I took a shaky breath and stepped through the mouth.

The floor squelched with slime and moisture making it slippery. I braced myself against one of the cave walls. Surprisingly, the wall heated my hand and its worn, smooth side glistened.

The tunnel sloped gently downhill. The light got brighter the further down I went. After several minutes, I approached a large opening into a cavern. The light came from the walls of the cavern which appeared to be covered in incandescent mucus that glowed in a brilliant bluish-green. All sorts of items, from backpacks and tents to books, moss-covered branches and discarded clothing, littered the floor. A thin sheen of slime covered everything. Bleached bones stuck out at different angles. Dozens of the slug-like creatures gathered in the center of the cavern. I crept closer moving from stack to stack of abandoned sundries.

The slug beings clustered together in a half-circle around the prone and mushroom-covered form of Paul. Only the rise and fall of the toadstools on his chest showed he still lived. The slugs murmured to each other in a quiet rasping tone punctuated at times by high-pitched whistles. A disturbance came from the back of the cavern and the high-pitched whistling grew louder and more frantic. The slugs glided backward.

From out of the darkness came a nightmarish creature. It was a squat batrachian thing. Dark green-almost-black skin with mottled patches of gray stretched over its bloated body. Yellowish eyes like pus peaked out from hooded lids and sat atop dark thick lips. A crown of twisted metal sat upon its head. It shambled toward Paul's body.

The grotesquerie opened its mouth and a fat scarlet tongue pocked with sores flicked out, licking its rubbery lips. A croak escaped my throat at the same time the toad king spoke. Its voice sounded almost human with a burbling quality to it. It weighed on my soul with its heaviness.

"What have you brought me, my pretties?"

The slugs went through an act alongside a reply and the lips of the toad king grew wide in a wicked distorted smile.

"I accept your tribute."

I knew I must act before that thing took Paul into its malignant embrace. I reached into the muck and pulled out a shredded hiking boot. I stayed low and hurled the boot into a far corner of the cavern. It struck a precariously balanced pile, scattering it to the floor, causing a loud commotion. The effect on the crowd was immediate with the slugs moving toward the sound and the toad king bounding backward.

I moved opposite of the distraction and shuffled from pile to pile as close to Paul as I could without leaving the safety of cover. I slowly reached out to grab Paul, but hesitated. Something disrupted the shadow where the toad king's bulk was concealed. I peered into the darkness. When my eyes became accustomed, two rheumy slits looked back at me. The toad king sensed my presence and waited for me to make my move.

The pile in front of me hid my exact location. I scanned it to see if anything could be used as a weapon. A large femur bone stuck out from the junk. Though I loathed to touch it, it was the only thing usable. I grasped the heft of it and slowly crawled out from my cover to Paul's body. I kept my eyes on the dark spot where the toad was waiting while scraping the mushrooms and toadstools from Paul's inert body.

Without warning the toad king leapt forward. Its massive tongue shot out of its vast mouth. I rolled to the side a fraction before the tongue lashed. I sprang at the toad with the bony weapon held in two hands over my head. The toad's head whipped to the side and the protruding tongue buffeted my side. I sailed through the air and hit the ground. The wind had been driven forcefully from my body. The end of the bone shattered in the crash. I gingerly picked myself up and faced the toad king.

Its yellowed eyes showed a cruel and brutal intelligence. Its tongue flicked out again. I spun around, avoiding it and rushed toward its bulk. I vaulted the stirring body of Paul, driving the spiked end of the bone straight down into the spongy head of my adversary. The bone penetrated the toad king's head and impaled its tongue into the floor of its mouth. It tried to croak, but only a gurgling issued forth. Its body shook violently, then went slack.

I slid from its back and collapsed to the floor, exhausted and in shock. Paul coughed fiercely. I crawled to him and surrounded him with my arms. We sat there, confused and relieved, until a sound caused us both to look around. The slugs had returned and regarded us with their black eyes and tight, round mouths.

Paul let out a shriek and scuffled backward, bumping into the dead toad king. His eyes and his mouth opened wide, but no sound issued forth. His mind was close to breaking. I limped back to him and pulled the bone from the toad's corpse. I turned back toward the slugs that were now formed in a semi-circle around us. They murmured in their low raspy voices.

I tensed, ready to pounce when the slugs opened their mouths as one. The noise that emerged sounded like a choir of cherubs and echoed throughout the cavern. The luminous sludge on the walls grew brighter as pictures emerged from the detritus under the light. It showed the story of the slugs, how they lived in peace and harmony in the cave until the toad came and subjected them all to its will. The toad king made them slaves, forcing them to take oblivious hikers as they slept. Now that the toad king's rule ended, they were free to live as they once did.

The slugs finished their chorus and slid aside, giving us free passage out. I helped Paul to his feet after he recovered from his shock. We exited the cave, walked nearly ten miles in a daze without stopping until we reached a highway and made it safely back to our car. When I got home, I scrubbed myself raw in the shower, but the scent of swamp and decay never left. Even now when I dream, I hear the murmuring of slugs and the deep insidious croaking of toads.

Jester Briefs (Rickey Rivers Jr.)

1.

Laughter is a great thing, the best thing. I like tears too. When I was young I was actually funny. I used to make people laugh all the time. I got old. I got tired. The three gongs before dying are tired, fat and cynical. At least they are if you see death as simply wasting away, becoming nothing and that's what plenty of people do after school. They waste away at a dead end job they hate until they retire. They retire and reflect. They cry in their graves. In this case the grave can be a home. Homes are nothing but walls and a roof. You lie within the walls and reflect. You do same thing in a box.

We all become ghouls eventually, just reflecting on our past: who we used to be, so far from glory the past might as well be a dream. And it does seem dream-like to reflect on childhood thoughts, moments and situations which mean so little in the present, but at the time were just the most important things in the world. Our view of the world is funny in older age light.

I remember scraping my knee outside the barbershop, it hurt me so bad. I looked at my bloody knee and cried. Dad stood there watching. Finally, he said "You're all right." True enough I was, but that wasn't the point. The point was at the time that knee scraping was just the most terrible thing. This is kid me reflecting, it's not like I haven't been hurt other times, worse times.

I got into a car accident in my teens. The back of my neck was fine for a while until it wasn't. Now any reflection on the crash is a crick in the neck, a painful flurry of stabbing sensations. But we all reflect and live on reflecting and trying to move on while the past moves ever closer. We wish the past to stay where it was. We want that, we desperately need the past to stay there, to be hidden in some dreamlike subconscious. But sometimes the past simply rises. Sometimes it boils over.

***

I reconnected with an old friend a few weeks back. He told me how much his life had changed. He used to be addicted to pills. It nearly led him to the grave. He told me he had a son now and a wife too. I was happy for him. He was always a good person. He just got caught up in the wrong things, the wrong crowd. The wrong crowd seems to always be just around the corner. It's always possible for any kid to randomly stumble upon a crowd of people wanting you to harm yourself, charm yourself into the warm wrappings of the drug life.

Of course the wrappings aren't warm, but it's a nice way to say you've been coerced into doing the unthinkable, what your parents would be ashamed of. Speaking of, my friend told me about a girl we went to school with. Apparently she's doing videos online stuffing inanimate objects into her body. It's some form of fetish and she gets paid well. I asked him how he knew and he said that she was online under a different name, but she has the same face.

77

Then I reworded my question. I asked him why he knew when he knew he had a wife. My friend went quiet for a while.

The point is my friend must have been looking in the wrong places to stumble upon videos of that nature. If you like porn that's fine. Say you like it and wanted a break from your wife. I wouldn't have judged him. We all need a break, away from the struggle of life, the toil on the body and the mind. It's okay to look outside your life for pleasure or whatever other kicks you need. I didn't even ask for the net name of the girl from school, it didn't matter. Names are just names. You can toss them away. The person after all is what needs to stay.

My friend is still my friend, of course I know his name, but his name doesn't matter. He's just a man with a wife and a kid. That's all he is and the girl from school is somewhere stuffing herself with objects for the amusement of degenerates. Her name, real or otherwise, is superficial. What matters is what she's doing with her life. It matters what we're all doing. We're all waiting for something to happen at the end of the day, some sort of interruption to make it all worth living. I think that's why people latch onto religion. They want it all to be worth it, to not get to the end and find out it's all been meaningless, a bubble of people waiting for a grand pop of nothing.

That's probably why I like laughter. It's fun to laugh loud and let tears fall from your eyes like gumdrops from a machine. We're all pretty much made to be machine-like we just break down from time and time, go to funerals for other machines and wait for science or grave robbers to sneak off with the machine parts. I guess that's a little sci-fi. People used to actually grave rob frequently. It's still a thing too. You can find videos online of people stealing parts from cemeteries. And all I can say is why not? Live and let die after all.

2.

Intertwining the cathartic crying with laughter I listen to my friend chatter on about his happy life of wife and kids. It's kids now because his wife is pregnant. They've been in the bedroom trying for another. Congrats to them. Thank goodness we have sex to produce little humans who'll go on to be abused. Not necessarily, by the parents, but by life itself. That's all life is made for after all. The first thing you do is get yanked out of a grown woman. Imagine seeing yourself pulled out of giant and everything is wet and then some man in white is slapping you on the bottom.

"The baby's crying from the pain, it's normal! Hooray!"

I know that's a reductive way to see it, but it's funny too. Imagine the kid hitting back? "Unhand me doctor!"

I think about that sometimes when I think about childbirth and I think about childbirth a lot. It's disturbing to produce a child, like removing waste from a rectum. Did you know that some woman actually vacate their bowels on the labor table? Imagine a baby sliding into that, a free fall straight into excrement, a water slide right into life.

And I had to look up what the table was called, originally I wrote 'birthing table' which sounds like the ancient history way to say it.

"Bring madam to the birthing table. It's time to rid her body of the hell spawn."

Or maybe that sounds like a group of nuns tending to a woman who's been violated by some demon in the dark alleyways of the streets, the place where no good people live and only bad people thrive and we couldn't possibly consider the child to be anything but a spawn from hell, because the child was forced into the woman.

So why consider the rights of a child who's not fully formed, who can't really talk? Who's not really here? Why consider a baby's opinion? Adults have deemed the baby to not even be a baby yet, and even in life the opinion of a child is worth less than, even when that child is screaming for a person to stop hurting or touching them. Adults don't care. They keep going.

"I'm authority, listen to me."

Authority has hurt many people, children and others, and yes children are people even if we adults deem them unworthy of opinions. They still live and breathe and think. They're people.

***

I recently went to the store and while waiting in line I saw this woman treat her son as less than anything but a nuisance. She pulled on his arm, spanked his bottom and called him names. I distinctively remember hearing her say "Stop acting a fool!" and "Nappy headed bastard" under her breath.

Once hearing the last insult I wished to have nine lives. In all but one of them I tortured her slow. I thought about that in the store. It made me smile. In one of my lives I treated the woman like a street urchin waiting in the shadows of an alleyway. I pulled out a long, inanimate object and shoved it down her throat. Next this same object went into her anus and the other place close to birth. I shook myself away from these thoughts once I heard "Next costumer!"

Finally, the woman and the child had left. I felt for the boy. He was only a boy. He wasn't to blame for much beyond wanting the simple pleasure of chocolate candy. After all that was the cause of the name calling: a block of candy, a treat for a child. Then the mother went naming calling, the use of bastard, the use of fool, the slandering of nappy hair.

All ridiculous things, the fool is to be respected, the fool after all entertains the kingdom. Where would the king and queen be without the fool to lift their spirits? And bastard as in insult is a terrible thing, after all it's not the fault of a child to be born to parents who weren't together. But we blame children for so much, even down to the nappy hair on their heads. I never saw nappy as an insult. The word never offended me. I like nappy hair. I like my hair. I don't think we should all have the same bit of hair on our heads.

Nappy hair is beautiful. I like how it curls and bounces. To deny a child the pleasure of enjoying their wonderful hair makes you a terrible mother.

You should be punished. Someone should take you deeply into an alley and treat you like the nun, treat you like the girl from school my friend told me about. But never pay you. You don't deserve payment. You deserve mistreatment because you dare slander a child born from you and insult the very hair produced from you. That nappy hair is yours too.

You're not better than your child because you chose to cover your head. You're not better than me. If I were multiple men I'd pull in different directions.

3.

I think back on times in school, being mocked for my supposedly nappy hair. The hair in question was an afro. I liked my afro too, it suited me. A group of girls mocked my hair. It didn't actually make me feel much, but I remember the mocking so maybe I'm wrong about how much it affected me.

Sometimes I think we bury a lot within ourselves and it peeks out from time to time. We shun all the bad moments to the back of our heads, but the moments don't disappear. They're just hiding in the deepest, darkest parts of our heads. They're little bats in the cave. They could come out if they wanted to. Maybe that was just a bat crawling toward the front of the cave when I saw that woman mistreat her child in the store. Maybe it was only anger telling me that I should use nine fictional lives to hurt her. The same way I wished, in retrospect, to hurt the girls who teased me.

And it was only teasing after all, nothing serious. It's always nothing serious when girls tease boys. Some girls even tease because they don't understanding their feelings. They tease because they actually like the boy and wish to express it. Thing is, they express this liking in mocking ways, and somehow the boys are blamed for not understanding intentions.

Several times I've been confused at bullying. People mocked me or teased me and it turned out they actually liked me in some way, somehow. This is not how to love. I never understood the mocking and teasing and hitting some gave back in the day. I didn't see them as love taps or love bites. I saw them as another child hurting me and trying to make me angry. So naturally I was an angry child. I was angry due to others.

***

I grew up well. My parents were great. School was the issue, other little boys and girls not knowing how to express themselves so they resorted to fighting and mockery. I hated school. I sometimes thought about terrible things in the classroom and some of the teachers encouraged the bull because they wouldn't actually punish the bullies.

Why do teachers run to the rescue once the bullied child fights back? I hated that. It stopped me from defending myself, the so called 'zero tolerance rule.' Now in my later years I see that I should have. I should have defended myself against the entire school. Instead I reduced myself to clown, a class clown, a court jester.

"If I make them laugh, they can't bully me."

That was my thought process. As I child I had to defend myself against the bull by being a jokester.

Maybe I shouldn't say 'I should have defended myself against the entire school' either. It's not like I didn't have friends. Of course, I had friends but they had their own lives. I don't know if any of them knew I was being bullied. I didn't talk about it, not even with my parents. Why would I? No one would do anything. And I had no time for "just tell the teacher." Like the teachers would actually care. Some of them were bullies too.

***

I sometimes wonder what happens to the bullies after school. They don't all go on to be murdered. Some of them live happy, healthy lives with nine spouses and children. Some of them become police officers and doctors and lawyers too. Bullies are everywhere all the time and no one talks or cares about it. It's seen as another part of growing up. Apparently you're supposed to just 'get over it' too. Not all of us do. Some of us hold on to the pain of the past. Sometimes that's all you can do.

Sometimes the pain of the past keeps you going, keeps you alive. Imagining all the pain you could cause another, to inflict what they gave to you tenfold. What a beautiful thought.

***

I have to admit something about my rantings of the nun from earlier. That's fiction. I know nothing of that fictional crime. I don't mean it's impossible for such a thing to happen. I just mean that my example was an example, that's all. Of course I don't want nuns to be hurt.

I remember going to the store and seeing an Amish woman shopping. She reminded me of a nun. It was strange to see an Amish woman in that setting. Something about the attire was interesting. She also seemed afraid, or timid. She was talking to herself trying to find a certain juice. I suggested something but I don't think she heard me, or maybe she ignored me. Maybe I was too brutish or aggressive sounding, which is funny because I have a light voice. I'm soft spoken. But maybe it's uncouth to speak to others outside the community even when it comes to matters of juice. Or maybe that's my own way of trying to make sense of the woman. She was older. She was maybe someone's mother. Which is a great thing, a child needs a good one. A person needs a good spouse.

I think about this woman sometimes. How she contrasts with other women. I try to compare her with the girl my friend spoke about, the one shoving things into herself. I can't compare them well. In my head it doesn't make sense. It's like they're different species. This is the same in comparison with the woman in the store mistreating her child. All of these women are women and yet I can put them in boxes. I can see how one has value over the others. I can see how one would deserve grace. I'm not religious, but if I were, I'd surely save the virtuous woman in the store, this nun of another culture. I would surely save her soul.

**

After all this writing I know what you may think. I know your judgment is clear. But you don't know me. You just know what I've given you. I think it's been nothing. I've only written down my thoughts and feelings. I've cracked myself open like an egg. It's important to be transparent. I have no need to pretend. I know who I am. I understand how life can change a person, but I always was a good child. I was always just waiting for something else, beyond violence, beyond sex. I was always waiting for love.

I briefly spoke of my parents being good, they were, they never hurt or teased me. I loved them. I truly did. I want to love others in the same way. I want to not think about the past as it was. I want the future to be much better, brighter. I want to want life. Is that wrong? I don't think so. I think we all want something out of life and it's sometimes hard to express.

I hope you get something out of this writing, even though I've given so little detail. Names don't mean anything, remember that. Names are what we're assigned. What matters most is what you do with your life and how you choose to live. Are you helping or hurting others? I understand why I'm here. I'm here to help. I understand why you wanted some sort of confession from me. But I have nothing to confess, if not only the following: I confess to being hurt.

I confess that the word 'sociopath' doesn't make sense. I confess that people do things for reasons and it's not just because they don't care about human life. I think that's a lie. I think people try so hard to group others into societal norms so that their actions make sense to them. Here's the thing, my actions do make sense. I don't act on impulse. I've always considered everything before I did it. That's why I didn't fight back as a child. That's why I didn't attack the woman in the store. I did life right. I've lived right. I moved freely through life, with my worries, like any other person. But I chose not to act on impulses. I confess to wanting love. That's all I've wanted. I don't wish harm on others. I can't control their actions. I can barely control my own. With this writing I'm sure you'll see that life has yielded me choices, and I've taken those choices. I'm sane.

Thunderbolts and Lightning
(Victoria Nangle)

19 October, 2019

You know the edge of clouds? The very edge of them. The bit where – when we were small and painting pictures, the blue of the sky always bled over into the white of the paper we'd carefully outlined in pencil as a cloud. What if that edge wasn't just an ocular illusion formed in graphite but a real, honest-to-God line. A boundary? What if?

My Gran told me that my great-grandfather – her father – got his family out of Russia on the last train as the revolution saw the fall of the Czar. Great-grandpa jumped onto the train engine and accosted the driver with gold in one hand and a gun in the other. Whichever of the two would make the driver hold the train for his family, he said, that was the one that he would use. Like something out of the Wild West, only in the Wild East. He was a great shmoozer and had connected with the Russian Royal family. And his passport – which hung proudly in Gran's dining room – had his occupation, rather ambiguously, as 'agent'.

The sights he must've seen. The fears he'd witnessed. Thinking about it, from the perspective of some of the most privileged people ever to exist, they were teetering to fall from one of the highest ivory towers in the world. Only 120 years previously they'd seen what had happened in France to their royals when the chasm between the haves and the have nots got too big. What if that ever happened to them? What if.

When my Gran died in 2012 the house was in disarray. My grandfather had passed away the month before and along with him the last semblance, it seemed, of any reason my grandmother had to hang on to the real world. Her dementia encroached and on Valentine's Day morning she crumpled into the live-in carer's arms and went to join him.

Leaving us with a treasure hunt with no clues.

She hid things. I don't just mean secrets like most people have, but literally a silver teapot under the floorboards of the downstairs lav. There were hiding places all over the house, and – due to some bad behaviour of another family member in recent years – the home we loved was mortgaged up to the hilt and creditors were calling.

Gran's family had travelled through Germany at the fall of the mark and arrived in New York in the run up to the Great Depression. Rumour had it my great-grandfather was a gambling man leading to opulence one day and stripped back necessities the next. I remember her telling me as a child to sew a pocket into my underwear to keep my money in, so that nobody could steal my savings. I just wriggled a little in embarrassment at the prospect of a shopkeeper seeing my knickers when I went out to buy my Cola bottles and left my pockets on the outside of my clothes.

But that was where she came from and why my aunt, my uncle, my mother, my brother and I found ourselves carefully tapping at every wall, floorboard and back of a wardrobe and sock drawer for hiding places and rescuing heirlooms before the beloved house went on sale and they were lost to us forever.

I remember I was recovering various family photographs from under the clear glass top of Gran's dressing table. Underneath a snapshot of my brother and I playing in the child-sized caravan at the end of the garden was where I found a tracing paper-thin single sheet of paper. A letter from my great-grandfather to a Major G Stanley of British Intelligence, dated 25 February 1921. And I can't say for sure if it was genuine but it was certainly old and for some reason Gran still had it and had hidden it. And Great-grandfather hadn't sent it because it was here. This is what it said:

'Dear Sir,

As related to you by the passport office, I was present in the Baltic Provinces, Vladivostock and Manchuria earlier in this year. I was also in Petrograd in 1917, which the passport office may have also informed you of – noted for point of control study. In all instances I witnessed the meteorological phenomena we discussed, it being most pronounced in Petrograd. Understandably, considering the events that took place under the Czar's fears if we are to consider our hypothesis possible.

The visual event that appeared as lightning and we now suspect to be a fissure between worlds, measures to have grown minutely but steadily in Manchuria at the last count, with an estimated time of arrival for the Realisation being the end of this decade or – at latest – the start of the 1930s. It is to this end that I recommend that we attempt to calm relations with Japan or begin our withdrawal from the province.

Yours truly, J.M. Jessiman Esq.'

On the dressing table, underneath the studio photo of my mother as a teenager, I found another wafer-thin sheet of correspondence. And another behind my grandfather's Royal Air Force portrait. So thin they could have feasibly been carbon copies of originals.

Together the titbits of information created a collage of a story. A theory of wars, conflicts, and misrule – in short created by the realisation of men's fears. A realisation that came into being when deepest unflinching dread, anxiety and suspicion was loud – literally with eyes staring boldly - in the presence of the fissures in the sky, or lightning. What was reported as storms of the time was – possibly - the thinning of the membrane between here and there, 'There' being a place where to fear it was to know it to exist. To *make* it exist. And the fears latched onto were not just of the man in the street, scared to go home because he'd get a bollocking for being late. Which he did. But also of rulers, emperors, presidents... and even a czar. Potentially.

After we'd finished searching for any last minute stashed gold doubloons hidden by my grandmother, I went home and hit the books. In 1931 Japan annexed what was then known as Manchuria, triggering years of conflict with China. I mean, it's sad and difficult but wars happening for all manner of reasons. Certainly not because someone stared at lightning.

91

I dug a little deeper. The Russian Revolution was brewing for years before 1917 saw the rise of the Bolsheviks and the Soviet Union. And the struggles of The Great War certainly would have cooked up a landscape ripe for bubbling over. But also on record, there was the weather.

In January and February 1917 it was noted that the temperature in Petrograd and Moscow was particularly cold and stormy. My great-grandfather's passport, his letters, family legend – all have him there then. Seeing fissures in the sky. In February 1917.

It had to be some mad conspiracy theory cooked up by the Allies to wrong-foot their enemies. So I decided to approach the idea from the other side. The first major weather that I can remember: the Great Storm of 1987.

My memory is of my brother waking me up for school and telling me that there'd been a hurricane in England and not believing him. Of walking to school because the tube wasn't running and dashing past trees that still stood erect by the side of the road, screaming with excitement that we had escaped the danger that it might've fallen on us. And it might've. I also remember my grandfather, a timber merchant, saying that a lot of fences would have to be replaced and that a lot of lumber might just flood the market. An estimated 15 million trees came down that night. But it was just a storm. With lightning.

Three days later there was a global stock market crash. Look it up if you don't believe me. The American market fell by 22.6 per cent in one day. By the end of the month the Hong Kong market had dropped by 45.8 per cent. They called it Black Monday. How many stockbrokers lived in London with me that year and happened to be looking up at the skies as they flashed with light, a chasm of brightness asking them for their deepest fears? How many investment bankers spoke back when the edge of the cloud opened and beckoned in their worries?

Storm-chasing. My great-grandfather had taken his family into the eye of the danger following the slashes in the sky, heralding disasters. It was no chance that my Gran had witnessed so much history. Or that a gambling man had steered them directly into it.

I'm not saying global warming doesn't exist, because it clearly does – despite Donald Trump's denials. But we have had had a lot of storms in recent years. A lot of bright light at the edge of cloud, blinding any onlooker with a twisted clown's grin of a smile. And our fears, the worries that have hidden under the beds of our minds, of Nazis legitimised, polar caps melting, Far Eastern despots with trigger-happy fingers, danger on the streets, a callous government dismissing the vulnerable, disbelieving the assaulted and prejudiced against, endangered animals hunted for sport... Every fear is now no longer hiding but instead at the forefront of minds looking up and marvelling at the bright light in the sky. It's in the clickbaited news, at the forefront of our minds. The stormy, dark and tempestuous sky.

Thunderbolts and lightning, very, very frightening. Another reason to blink tightly against the bad weather.

You probably noticed that there was a storm last week. Great big walls of electricity lit the sky, with snaps of it all over Facebook hoping to be spotted for some previously unknown nature photography prize.

I was a bit angry as it struck, as it goes. I'd had a day of it. My feet were soggy from the incessant rain; the British prime minister and the US president were doing my head in to such an extent I visibly flinched every time a story came up on my news feed detailing a new feat of idiocy.

I am frequently infuriated by the lack of statesmen in politics, replaced by an overflowing ant hill of wannabe reality stars with nanny-complexes. It's all very well declaring the myth of the grown-ups, that none of us are really adult – just old, but when no one steps up too many fall down. That calls for anarchy. For revolution. Tear it down and start again, as the song goes.

I stared at the sky, out to sea, fury in my eyes. I felt the flash across my face and saw the waves light up, their own tempers illuminated across the horizon with white horses stampeding towards the shore, the wind whipping my wet hair into my eyes. My eyes wide open in defiance.

This morning I read an article online that said behind anger, there is fear. But it's just weather. And my great-grandfather was a chancer with an eccentric bent, shared by my grandmother, his letters discovered in haste and in grief. Right.

Postscript
9 June 2020

I shared this story at a Halloween event last year. Stood on a stage to half a dozen people and let it be known. Hardly viral but out in the world. About a month later I sent it to a publisher friend, who sent it to their publishing partner – just to get their take on the words of the thing. They were in Venice for a work 'event'. St Luke's Square was flooded, water was washing in under the front door of their hostel and great sheets of blinding light were illuminating the sky. I thought it was 'sweet' when she emailed that she'd felt chills down her back when she read the words, holed up in that whirlpool.

This morning I was wryly addressed as 'Cassandra' in a text from the producer of that Halloween performance show. I've not seen him in months but my story had stayed in some lizard-brain part of his mind.

After Venice's flooding was the Australian bushfires, covering the continent in flames.

Last week saw my first days back to office work after months of being furloughed by the government. Pub visits are virtual now and seeing someone's legs a surprise treat after a financial quarter of Skype and Facetime calls that cuts us off mid clavicle. It also witnessed the second week of global demonstrations in the name of #BlackLivesMatter, growing and growling after years of being told to 'wait'.

And it's only June. I'd love you to check the history books for the rest of this year, People Of The Future. The weather reports, too – if you have a fancy. We all wear masks now, to stop the spread of the virus. We've learned to sew them. I sew –

who'd've thought it? I sew masks and stuffed toys and headscarves and blackout curtains. You might want to pick up the skill yourself.

The Tourist in London (Dorothy Davies)

He was just like any other mark, you know? Scruffy sort of guy, tweed jacket, slacks with not much of a crease, bit of a stubble thing going on. Balding a bit but who isn't? Big nose, I remember the big nose. Washed out sort of eyes, not much colour there. Looked like he hadn't got two pound coins to rub together, if I were truthful with you.

He gets in the cab at Liverpool Street Station, wants a trip round London.

OK, I says, let's go! Where do you wanna start, sir?

He says, that thing near the river, that tall thing you see from the sky.

I says, do you mean the Monument?

He says, I do that.

So we goes to the Monument. I sits in the cab while he climbs the 300 odd steps to the top, I sees him go round the viewing platform, I wait while he climbs back down the 300 odd steps and I think, rather him than me. I'd rather sit here in comfort, off me feet, watching the meter tick on. This is the good one; I remember thinking, the rare good one. The one we all talk about getting and few of us do. Go round London seeing all the sights. Usually from the windows, mind you, this one was different, getting out to see places, leaving the meter running.

Oh be sure I kept the meter running. I might have had Princess Diana in my cab and I would have kept the meter running. Fat chance of that, before or now. Oh but I loved that woman... Enough! Just gotta say no one would have made me drive that fast and kill the one true beauty who walked our planet. Oh hell, here I go again...

Forget it. Let's get back to the weird one.

I've been driving a cab in London all my working life, me. Love it, I do, all the people, the sights you see out the window along the streets, them's as wanna talk to you about London and all it has to offer, them as hates it, only here on business or 'cos they gotta be.

Not this mark, though, he was - different.

He wanted the Tower next, so we went to the Tower. And I sat outside and waited while he did the tour round, seeing those – what do you call them, the ones in the outfits? Can't remember. Anyway, he went there.

He wanted the London Eye after that, wanted to see, what was that strange new building called? Can't remember. Well, we went there.

He wanted Buckingham Palace, wanted to see the – damn it, where's my memory gone! The men in red outfits and tall hats? Well, we went there.

And we went on like that. All day we went round and round London and all day... I just realised... my memory got worse and worse till I could hardly remember how to get from one place to the other. Like I was in a fog, you know?

And come to think on it, he got –

Smarter and smarter as the day went on, clothes got better, he got more hair, he got less beard. His eyes got more colour. And I got – older.

And I forgot things. It was like – he was some kind of vampire and he was draining me of all my knowledge.

Next thing I know he's driving the cab and I'm in the back, watching the world go by, wondering where the hell I am.

We went back to the Monument and I got out and he drove off. I opened the door and climbed up the 300 odd steps to the top and when I got there, I thought, how odd, he said 'the thing you can see from the sky.' How did he see it from the sky, I asked myself. And I asked myself who he was to drain me like that.

I found myself on the viewing platform of the Monument and everyone who came up walked right through me and I knew I wasn't human any more.

Then I realised he wasn't human either or he wouldn't have been able to take over like that and put me in the back of my own cab and then drive off in it and I'm lost, lost, lost and only you've seen me in the last ten years.

I'm right bored with the view, but that ain't the real problem.

It gets damn lonely up here, I can tell you.

So, what d'ya wanna talk about?

Closing The Deal (Diane Arrelle)

The President of the United States lay on his deathbed. Contentment from an adulthood filled with satisfaction and joy overwhelmed the fear ruining his last moments of life. Fear, once just a nagging doubt over choices made in a distant past, was now foremost.

From another room the ever eternal news was broadcasting his life story. "Alexander Thomas, the most beloved of presidents of the 21st century was thought by many to be the wisest, is not expected to live beyond the next few hours. Paralyzed last week by a series of devastating strokes, he is surrounded by his wife, six children and fourteen grandchildren."

The newscaster's voice droned on as Alexander struggled to hold onto life. "Thomas served two four-year terms as president before retiring to live on the family estate in Maryland. He has spent the last three decades raising his famous thoroughbred horses and lecturing on the world affairs that he did so much to shape. Historians agree that Alexander and his Secretary of State, the late Eric Devlin, managed to bring the world to the brink of peace and beyond. A peace we are still basking in twenty-eight years later. At age eighty-five, Thomas awaits the end calmly and at peace with his maker. A great man who will be missed."

Alexander Thomas waited to greet Eric again after living more than sixty years of the good life. He wished his body were capable of laughing for he was laughing on the inside-perhaps a bit bitterly-at the phrase, "at peace with his maker." He'd never met his maker and doubted he ever would. So, at peace or not, he was going to pay the piper. His only hope was that the good he had accomplished would weigh in his favor.

Maybe I'll be forgiven, he thought with a small glimmer of hope and closed his tired eyes. He sighed deeply and stopped breathing. His frail heart fluttered to a stop and the last sounds he heard were someone softly sobbing and the long flat beeeeep of the monitor.

A puff of sulfurous smoke appeared before him as he rose up, leaving his human remains prone on the bed. As the wispy vapor took form, Alexander gave a weak smile and said, "Hello Eric, long time no see."

The young auburn haired man gave a wide toothy grin. "You really think a measly thirty years was a long time? Just wait till you get a load of eternity!"

Alexander looked around the three-hundred-year-old room one last time. "Kind of hard to leave behind, you know," he said wistfully. "So what happens now, does everything disappear in blast of fire? And what about my family?" he had an edge of panic in his voice.

"Nope, the house stays, the seventy-five acre ancestral home remains, your fictitious history as well as the family's actual history stays on the books and tell me honestly, do you really care if all those brats and grandmonsters of yours live or die?" Eric started to laugh convulsively. "You... you... didn't give a damn last time! G... g... et it, didn't give a... a damn!" he sputtered.

"Last time was a life ago," Alexander said softly and blinked away the flashing memory of four dirty, uncouth children, four terrified, screaming children, four children plummeting to their death. Shuddering involuntarily, he muttered, "And it was worth it!"

"Ya think so, huh?" Eric said, bringing the laughter down to a nasty smile. "Well look, it's been fun gabbing but I got a lot of scum to pick up and deliver. So let's go."

Alexander was transported in a puff of foul-smelling vapor to a luxurious room trimmed and furnished in wood and leather. It smelled of lemons and fine wax. He settled into a comfortable, warm chair and was amazed that he had the sense of smell and touch. An elderly gentleman dressed like a butler bowed in his direction, "Brandy, Sir?" he asked. "There is quite a wait, as there are several hundred ahead of you this afternoon."

"Several hundred?" Alexander asked with a frown.

The old man smiled condescendingly, "Excuse my saying, Sir, but you shouldn't get upset. After all, you do have all the time in the world and I don't think you really want to hurry this appointment. Now, about that brandy?"

Alexander nodded and found a crystal glass in his waiting hand. He took a sip and nodded to himself. "Hell, this isn't so bad at all."

"Ah, this isn't Hell. It's only your waiting room," a voice like Curly Howard's squeaked.

"Only the best for a great politician and a kind, loving, family man, you know."

Alexander looked up from his drink and found himself eye-to-eye with a short magenta creature with a mouthful of mismatched yellowed fangs surrounded by a squashed-in face. It scratched at the horns on its head with one hand and scratched at its pointed tail with the other.

"Hi," it said, spewing out breath so foul Alexander gagged and turned his head away. It vanished, appeared to his left, once again in front of his face. "Nah, nah, ya can't escape me!" it taunted. "I'm a demon and your personal counselor here in Purgatory. I'll be counseling you while you await judgment. It will only be a lifetime or two before the boss gets to your file so sit back and relax. I've brought the entertainment."

Alexander saw the wall across the room fade away and, like a video, he watched scenes unfold before him. It was his life, his life as Alexander Thomas rolling backwards from the grand funeral he had missed, to his death and back through his years of retirement as a blue-blooded gentleman farmer and respected elder statesman.

His life continued to unwind backwards. His eight years as President, his shining moments of glory as he maneuvered world leaders to accept his goal of world peace and unity as well as his global campaign to end worldwide polluting forever. He proudly watched his fights move on in reverse as he was elected president then as a senator, a governor and a mayor. It was difficult to see it in rewind, having him end as a college student at Yale. The picture faded away to gray.

103

The childhood everyone else in the world knew about never really happened. Alexander Thomas came into being at twenty-one. The Thomas' had been childless up to that point, but with the flick of a blood red pen, world history had been altered. No one in the entire world even blinked an eye, not even his new found family.

"Guess you think you're a good man, don't you?" the little demon said in an oily voice. "Bet you think saving the world will save your soul, huh? Well, watch what comes next and tell me about your worthiness."

With a barking laugh, the creature added, "I know that the only reason you were so righteous and good was just an act to save yourself. Yep, just a silly trick to get out of paying your dues. Well baby, it don't work that way here, you can bet your life on that!"

Alexander cringed at the words. They were partly true. He thought he could change his fate by being a good man, a really good man. Well, maybe the little guy was only trying to get him to make some kind of mistake.

"Why did Eric come to me and help save civilization, anyway?" He asked the question that had nagged at him for years. Eric had given him all the advice for global change. Deep down, he knew that through Eric, Satan had used him for his own means.

"Well baby, it wasn't to save your lousy soul. You would have made a mess of things just like every other mortal."

"Then why, tell me why, did you go to all that trouble?" Alexander asked. "After all, you're all supposed to be evil, why save the world?"

The demon giggled. "Well let's see," he said. "On the short end on the stick, it was funny to watch you try to change your true nature and become a good man. We all got a kick out of that."

The demon stopped for a moment to stare at Alexander with disgust. "Why do all you mortals think you can renege on a deal? Down here we may be evil, but we respect a contract. I guess you can say we are honest with our dishonesty."

The creature looked at his bare wrist then at the numbers flashing on the wall behind Alexander. It nodded and said. "Anyway, to answer your question about world affairs, we are evil but not stupid. We saw a chance to keep the status quo on earth and grabbed it. After all, good times for mankind means big business for us. When things go bad, humans turn to prayer. Next thing you know is we have a recession down here. The boss gets grumpy, we get quotas to fill and nobody is happy. Guess you could say our life is hell when things go bad.

"Look, the clock on the wall says we're coming up to your turn soon. Just a couple of decades to go," the demon said, looking past Alexander again. "So, let's finish up this travesty called your life."

The front wall faded again and when Alexander's life started to unfold it was moving forward. Alexander watched the all too familiar scenes from a life he thought had been erased forever. His birth to a family too big for the three room apartment in a rough and tough town near the shore. He watched an unhappy, little waif named

Paulie Winters drift from skipping school, to shoplifting, to robbing people's beach bags as they swam in the ocean, to dropping out of high school and joining a gang. He saw a smart little boy with brains and talents. Brains and talents that were going to be wasted on a life of petty crime and squalor. It was going to be a life cut short by disease, accident or murder. Any way he looked at it, he was facing a born loser, a loser by environment.

"Gets you right here, don't it?" the demon giggled as he patted his heart. "Poor little gutter snipe, didn't stand a chance at all."

"That's right!" Alexander snapped defensively. "That boy that lost me didn't get a fair shake at all. There was no way anyone could survive in a hell hole like that!"

"All your siblings did. In fact, your brother, Stanley, who was seven years younger than you, went on to college on a full scholarship. He became a prominent doctor and respected member of the community. He helped almost all his brothers and sisters get out of that life, the eight of you did all right.

"Nine," Alexander said.

"Nope, eight," the demon snapped. "You stopped existing to that family when you switched identities. Well, you certainly saved them a lot of shame and grief."

The show continued, and Alexander watched twenty-year-old Paulie knock-up Eleanor, a homely girl with two big brothers. Next thing he knew he was married, working in a convenience store at night and doing petty crimes on the side.

106

Alexander watched himself become a bitter and old man at twenty-five. He saw a man he hated to remember, a man he pitied, a man who would sell his soul for a chance to escape four dirty, horrid, screaming brats, an ugly, skinny, nagging, chain-smoking wife and a dead end life.

"Poor jerk," he muttered. "What a dumb putz!"

"Still is, if you ask me," a new voice said.

Alexander turned from the story of his life to find Eric back with him. "Come for the part you like best?" he asked.

"Yes," Eric answered. A look of rapture glazed his eyes. "This one was just too easy."

They watched as Paulie, the four pre-school-aged children and Eleanor sat in a July traffic jam on the Staten Island side of Brooklyn. As his old green Ford overheated and started spewing steam, they were rear-ended by a fiery red, pick-up truck.

Paulie jumped out of the car, ran back and started pounding on the door of the truck. "Open up, you stupid jerk!" he screamed, finally at the end of his rope. "Open up, you son of a bitch and fight like a man!"

The truck began to glow and Paulie jumped back, holding his hands in pain. He watched bug-eyed as the door opened, letting out curls of thick, grayish yellow smoke. Then Eric stepped out, dressed like a New York cowboy. "You got a problem, buddy?" he asked.

"Not anymore!" Paulie answered and took a swing at him. He missed and fell into the side of the truck. "How'd I miss you?"

"Like this!" Eric replied and vanished only to reappear a few feet away. "Neat trick, huh?"

"How'd you do that, man?"

"Well, you see, I'm a salesman," Eric explained. "I work for the big red guy down under?"

"What's Australia got to do with disappearing tricks?" Paulie interrupted.

"Look, dummy," Eric sighed. I work for Lucifer and I've got a deal for you."

"Yeah?"

"Yeah! Look, I can make you anybody you'd like if you'll trade me your soul. Now is that a deal or what?"

"You're telling me I could be President of the United States?"

Eric smiled, satisfied that the deal was going to be a piece of cake. "Yep. Would you like that?"

"Not with that family, I don't!" Paulie said pointing to his beat up car.

"We can handle that with no problem. So, do we have a deal?"

"Sure, you get rid of that bunch of losers and make me another person, make me President and you can have anything you want," Paulie said. "Hell, Hell can't be any worse than this!"

"Right you are, Buddy!" Eric said producing a red quill pen and contract from the air. "Just sign here!"

Paulie grabbed the pen and signed. "Well maybe you're nuts but I like the tricks and I ain't got nothing to lose. Now what?"

"Get back in your car and the future will take a new course. Just drive to your destiny and in 60 plus years, I'll see you in Hell!"

The contract, Eric and the truck vanished. Paulie shrugged and got into the stifling car. His wife lit up another cigarette, two of the kids started to fight and the traffic jam ended. The cars in front of him were gone and the Verrazano Bridge stood empty before them.

Paulie smiled and stepped on the petal, pushing all the way to the floor. The car hesitated, shuddered, then took off. They reached the top of the bridge only to find it gone. It had vanished from under them. The little crowded Ford fell through the shimmering summer air, slowly turning over and over as the family inside screamed in terror. Finally, it hit the Narrows, landing upside down and smashing its cargo to a watered-down red paste. Everyone died, except Paulie who suddenly found himself Alexander Thomas, son of wealthy and established blue-blooded, American aristocrats.

The wall went blank and Eric stood up. Entertaining show, wouldn't you say?" He studied Alexander with a frightening grin. "Well, well, the boss says it's time to go. Now let's just replay you're last words as Paulie Winters."

The wall faded back to the scene at the foot of the bridge. Paulie was looking at Eric and said, "...I ain't got nothing to lose..."

Alexander found himself sitting on the torn plastic seat of the green Ford. He looked around and felt sick with a dread more gut wrenching than anything he'd ever experienced before. He was choking on cigarette smoke that just hung in the motionless, ninety-four degree heated air. He had to cover his ears. Four little voices were shouting for attention.

"Gotta go bafroom!"

"He touched me!"

109

"She touched me first!"

Eleanor crushed out her cigarette stub and immediately lit another. The traffic backed up endlessly. Craning his neck, Alexander couldn't see the beginning of the traffic jam and looking back he couldn't spy the end. The smell of exhaust competed with the stench of sweaty bodies and baby shit.

"That's mine!"

"Are we there yet?"

"I gotta go Bafroom!"

"I'm gonna throw up!

And Eleanor crushed out her cigarette and lit another one. Horns blared all around them and the temperature rose another degree. Suddenly Eric was standing by the driver's window. "You once said Hell couldn't be any worse than this. Well, buddy, guess what? This is your hell!"

With a flash of smoke he was gone, leaving his laughter and final words to linger in the still, fly-infested air. "Welcome to eternity!"

Alexander laid his head on the steering wheel and sobbed.

"He touched me again!"

"Ma-ma-ma-ma-ma..."

"Daaad... make them stop!"

"I'm hungry!"

And Eleanor crushed out her cigarette and lit another one.

Dead City Blues (Paul Edwards)

Static.

Behind it, the ghost of a face; a figure in rain. I hear a voice, too:

"…All for you…"

I move the aerial around, but the TV jumps and hisses and I swear under my breath as I set the aerial back down again. "Almost got something."

Matilda doesn't reply. She's brushing her teeth while humming a lullaby Mum used to sing to us when we were young.

I twitch the curtains. "There's a man out in the street," I say, "lying on his side with his face turned away. I see blood running out from under him, trickling down the road in a rivulet."

I let the curtains flap back into place. "What shall we do with ourselves?" I turn, trying hard not to think about what I'd just seen. From the bathroom comes the steady sound of running water.

Matilda drifts out of the bathroom and stands before me in her pretty white nightdress. "You forgot to turn the tap off," I say, but she ignores me and hums that stupid lullaby through gritted teeth.

"We could try going home. Maybe Mum's not…" I cock my head. "You okay, Sis?"

Matilda coughs blood and it's then I realise I'm all alone in this world.

I press my hands to my face and shriek through my fingers. Matilda stumbles, eyes rolling wildly behind her hair.

I dash out the room, charge downstairs and push through the front door, running around the man lying inert in the road. I almost throw up, but I swallow it down and tumble through a gate into the silent confines of Locksley Cemetery.

Headstones and crosses stab out of the overgrowth. Angels stare at me with hollow eyes. I flit around open graves and push through the far gate, stepping back out onto the street. My old secondary school faces me, looking tired and decayed. Windows bare jagged glass teeth. Riotous weeds poke out of the tarmacked playground.

The day breathes. A discoloured Coke can rattles past. *I'm all alone,* I realise, but I mustn't cry, not yet; I dig my fingernails into the palms of my hands and hiss under my breath: "This isn't happening. This can't be real."

My gaze switches to the chimney stacks and shattered windows of the dead industrial estate opposite. The buildings are stained with soot, looking on the verge of collapse. Someone has spray painted words over the sign welcoming people into our town:

WELCOME TO DEAD CITY.

***

Sunlight scrapes away the shadows of the terraced houses along Foree Road.

I walk and walk, hands tightly clenched, not really thinking about where I'm going. I start believing this isn't real; that it's just a dream and I'll wake up in my room back in our house on

Sherman Drive to find everything normal again. But then I'm aware of the pain in my palms and tears prickle my eyes as I gaze upon the vicious half-moons imprinted on my flesh. I can't believe my sister has gone; I can't think of anyone else I can turn to now.

A wave of tiredness hits me – I flop down in a shop doorway and close my eyes. When I open them again, it's dark. A misshapen shadow stands in an orange pool of streetlight before me.

My heart thuds and thunders. I lever myself up using the doorframe, the moon dropping down all maggoty and cracked into my line of vision.

The figure lifts its head, its face a thin, pale oval. I dart around two abandoned cars, then charge out onto the main road where more figures turn to watch me pass. One of them stumbles out of a shop doorway and I scream, quickening my pace. Silvery-blue faces peel themselves from the darkness. I bite my lip and sprint to the *Robins* cinema, pushing through the double doors and up a narrow flight of stairs.

I turn down a corridor and enter the main screening room. The cinema screen is at the far end and before me are rows and rows of blood red seats. I hurry down the steps and squeeze into the space between the first and second rows.

The door into the main screening room bursts open and I duck down real quick.

Seconds pass.

Shit, I think. *Oh shit, shit*. I'm so scared I can barely breathe. I poke my head up just as a decayed woman looms over me, her skin crawling with worms. I scream so loudly I think my lungs might

113

burst, then her head explodes and bits of brain and gristle shower my face, clothes and hair.

"Fran!"

I look around, terror-stricken. A boy from my English Literature class at school, Stephen, approaches, clutching a smoking shotgun. He's always so neat and presentable, but now his clothes are torn and one of the lenses to his glasses is cracked.

"It's okay," he whispers, raising one of his hands in a placating gesture. "Everything's going to be okay."

Sammy-Lee, my best friend at school, told me that she'd heard rumours that Stephen fancies me. I remember this as he holds out his hand; I ignore it, using a seat instead to help me stand up. I run trembling fingers across my face. When I bring them away again, they're slick with blood.

Stephen's hand drops to his side. "We need to go."

"Where?" I say. "Where can we go?"

"There's a fire exit behind you. It'll take us down onto the street."

A loud moan fills the auditorium. I whirl and see more of those things shuffle slowly into the room. Stephen shoulders the door open and then we're scrambling out onto the fire escape and down a set of rusting stairs.

The precinct below is eerie and dark; most of the streetlights are out. Jagged pieces of glass hang like enormous knives from warped window frames.

"Look out," Stephen yells and I turn to see a face pour out of the shadows like milk. He fires his gun and the head explodes, showering us with pieces of skull and brain. I gag and retch violently.

Stephen grips my arm. "It's like Romero," he says in a hushed, reverent tone. "You know, the dead films? Night, Dawn, Day?"

I stare at him.

"You got to shoot them in the head. It's the only way to stop them."

The dead thing stumbles and falls sideways onto a sack of rubbish. "God," Stephen whispers, raking a hand through his hair. "Sorry, I'm not thinking straight." He looks me in the eye. "This isn't the movies. This is *real*."

More moans ring out across the night.

"Come on," he says, seizing my wrist, pulling me along. "There's a clothes store… I broke into it the other day. There's an exit at the back of the shop onto Cardille Road. So we won't be trapped there if they come for us."

I stare at the motionless thing on the floor. "*Come* on," he urges, tugging again on my wrist.

We hurry to the double doors of *Next* and he immediately smashes through them with his gun. Then we're inside, shutting, locking, barricading the doors.

We step away, gasping, panting, Stephen watching me fall back against the wall, his eyes unreadable behind his glasses. "The nights are the worst," he says at last, breaking the silence between us. "They're much more active at night. Plus, you don't see them. They seem to come out of nowhere. And if they scratch or bite you, you've had it – you become one of them."

I think of Matilda; of the stranger who had come up to her in the street and how he'd taken a bite out of her. I blink tears and fold a blind over the window. "You'll be okay," he says. "Stay with me and you'll be all right." He laughs, meekly. "You didn't look twice at me at school." His cheeks immediately colour. "It's okay, no one did. It's because... well, I'm different, aren't I? I didn't value the same things *they* did – like football and brand names on clothes." His shoulders sag. "It's no wonder they didn't last five fucking minutes when it all..." His eyes narrow into slits. "You okay?"

"Sure." I come away from the window, the blind popping back into place.

"Don't think we're safe here. We should think about bedding down for..." He stops as I drift over to a radio on a windowsill. I flick the power switch and interference fills the room.

"...what I can do... see me differently... who I really am... "

"Can you hear that?" I ask, wheeling, my eyes widening.

Stephen cocks his head, listening. "I've sat in front of that thing for hours. The TV, too. But I never pick anything up."

"I swear I heard something."

He flicks the power switch. "Ssh!"

"What?"

He nods to the window.

There are things moving out there, scratching the glass with their black, blood-caked nails.

"We need to get out of here," he says. "And fast."

116

We weave past a couple of mannequins and make our way to the back of the shop. I gasp when a giant shadow passes across the frosted pane of glass in the door. Stephen turns to me, pressing a finger to his mouth. Then he crouches and lifts the letterbox.

"There's one out there," he says.

He lets the flap down gently, then glances behind us. There's a fire-axe encased in glass on the wall. "Here," he says, pushing the shotgun into my hands. "I need to think about preserving ammo. I can take him with the axe – I know I can." He uses his elbow to break through the glass, then prises the axe free.

I gaze at the shotgun, smooth the shiny black barrels, the handle, fingertips flicking over the trigger.

"Get the door," Stephen hisses and I look up, nod and turn the handle. He kicks open the door and hollers as he steps outside, wielding the axe above his head. I see a stark-white face. Then the axe comes down and the dead thing crumples. "Got you," Stephen laughs, his twitching face covered in gore. "Got you, you fucker!"

I stare at the thing on the ground with the axe sticking out of it, then press a hand over my mouth.

Stephen turns to me, his eyes wide and wild-looking. "Go!"

We dart out the back alley and into a deserted residential area. Two streetlamps hum, coating the pavement with light. Stephen leads us down the side of a house and we come to some overgrown bushes. He glances behind us, ensuring there's no one there, then parts the foliage. I crawl in after him, bushes snapping shut behind me. We're in a secluded spot away from the street, where little can see or find us. I breathe out a sigh of relief.

Stephen reaches for an apple and I peer around, noticing small boxes of ammo, a machete, a pair of binoculars, a serrated knife, chocolate bars and a box of Ritz crackers.

A den.

"Want something?" he asks, but I shake my head. "Suit yourself."

I watch him eat. "Where did you find the gun?"

"It belonged to my Dad." He pulls the weapon close to him. "He had a license for it and everything."

"You always used to stare at me," I say, changing the subject.

Stephen stops eating for a moment. "Didn't think you noticed." Then, smiling shyly: "I... like you."

I don't know what to say to that.

"Doesn't matter anyway," he mutters through a mouthful of apple. "The past's obliterated. Whatever happened before... well, it's meaningless now."

"No," I mutter, tears springing into my eyes. "I mean, this *can't* be real. This is... madness!"

Stephen hangs his head. "I'll look after you," he says, quietly. "We can get through this together, right? Just as long as we *trust* each other."

"I'm tired," I say.

Stephen falls silent and I sit there with my eyes closed for some time. When I open them again, Stephen's curled up asleep and I watch his eyelashes flutter as he dreams. I close my own eyes and when sleep comes, it's punctuated by stark, frightening images:

A figure barely discernible behind static.

Matilda stumbling into a wall.

A mannequin's blank stare.

Broken fingernails scratching against glass.

A marble angel.

Stephen's bloodstained face. *I'll look after you.*

My eyes snap open and I gasp out loud. Dawn light filters into the den. Stephen is still asleep, his head cushioned by foliage. My attention is drawn to the shotgun in his lap and slowly, very slowly, I reach for it. Stephen murmurs and mutters and I stare at him for a moment, willing him still. Then he quietly begins to snore and I lift the gun and bring it up to my chest. I look around, spying the ammo in their little red boxes. I tip some of the cartridges out and stuff them into my jacket pocket. I pull back the bush where a thorn sticks into my thumb and I want to scream, to cry out, but my teeth clamp together and I crawl out of the darkness as quickly and quietly as possible.

Sunlight flares over the silhouettes of distant factories. I glance up and down the road but there's no one here. I race toward Cooper Lane, my footfalls echoing between rows of terraced houses. The new-born sun bleeds over torn tangles of barbed wire hanging from crumbling walls, stark against the scarlet sky like rows of shattered teeth.

Cooper Lane is, like every other street in the city, eerie and quiet. I try to remember the number of his house, glancing repeatedly up at the windows I pass by. Then I see red curtains and a dust-smeared pane and think – *that's it, that's the one.* I

119

remember Sammy-Lee pointing it out to me once when we were walking home from school.

I perch on a bench in the park opposite and have this crazy notion I can shape Stephen's face out of the clouds above. I blink twice, rapidly, then stare uneasily at the gun. I remember watching Stephen load it; he made it look so easy. I glance round to see one of those *things* shuffling about in a shop doorway on the other side of the road. I think about shooting it, but lower the gun and walk over to the house instead.

The garden gate sags on one rusted hinge. The front door is locked, but the patio doors around the back aren't. I slide them open and step carefully into the living-room.

The clock's stopped, galaxies of dust swirl through the air. I edge around furniture and enter the hallway. To my right, a flight of stairs leads up to the first floor. I grip the railing and ascend, shotgun clenched in my fist.

The floorboards creak beneath me as I step into Stephen's room. It's furnished with a single bed, a chest of drawers, a portable TV and DVD player and a lava lamp. Sellotaped to the wall is a poster for a movie, *Zombie;* beneath the picture of a maggot-ridden corpse are the words: *We are going to eat you.*

I drift over to a shelf stacked with DVDs and carefully run my finger along their spines.

Tombs of the Blind Dead. The Serpent and the Rainbow. Carnival of Souls. The Living Dead at the Manchester Morgue. Zombie Creeping Flesh. Dead and Buried. The Beyond. Burial Ground.

I pull open drawers. See magazines: *Dark Side, Fangoria, GoreZone.*

I turn and scream.

Stephen's watching me from the doorway. "What are you doing?"

"You," I hiss, pointing the gun at him. "I *knew* it. You've done this. All of this! You're controlling this somehow!"

He pales. "What…?"

"I-I don't know how you did it, but make it stop. Make it stop NOW!"

He shakes his head. "I don't know what you're talking about."

"I'm trapped in your sick fantasy, aren't I? You and me, to be *alone* like this; in this… *sick* and vile world! It's like I've walked into your head – into your *fucked-up* brain!"

"Fran…" He shuffles forward.

"Don't come any closer! I know what this is now. You want to look after me. Protect me. So that I…"

My hands are trembling, but I keep the gun trained on him.

"Please." He takes another step forward. "Give me the gun – we're not safe. I really don't…"

I pull the trigger, the shot blasting through the lens covering his left eye and spraying blood and brains across the wall behind him.

Silence.

I take several steps back, shaking, smoke billowing from both barrels of the gun.

"It's done," I whisper and a hoarse, crooked laugh escapes me. "The spell... it's broken. Broken and lifted at last."

I charge out of his room, rush downstairs and fling open the front door... only to see the thing in the doorway turn its bloodstained face toward me.

I cup a hand over my mouth.

I close my eyes.

I scream and scream.

You Know What They Say About Wishes... (Rie Sheridan Rose)

It was my Monkey Paw moment—you know that story, right? A couple gets three wishes from a mummified monkey's paw...what a nasty little talisman. They wish for the stereotypical money, even if it is a relatively modest amount by today's standards and the next day they receive the precise sum asked for in compensation for their son's death.

What a conundrum.

Of course, with her maternal instincts, the wife wants her son wished back again, despite the horrific mangling he received in the machinery of the factory he worked at. Hen-pecked papa complies when he can't talk her out of it, but comes to his senses at the sound of a knock at the door and wishes the young man back to his grave.

Since they never open the door, there's no way to know if they wasted those last two wishes or not. I kind of think not. But then, I have had some experience with wanton wishes myself.

It's really curious, isn't it? Our obsession with wishes—magic lamps with genies inside; magic monkey paws with fakir folderol attached; meteoric "falling stars" that we expect to better our lives. And yet, if the wishes ever do come true, it's 99% sure you will regret that they did.

You really do have to be careful what you wish for. I learned that lesson early, playing one of those role-playing adventure games with a sadistic Game Master who would freely give out wishes—but take full advantage of the least little mis-wording to make sure that you regretted using them. Wish for your weight in gold and receive it while you were swimming a deep river so that you drowned. That sort of thing.

So I thought I would be prepared if I ever stumbled upon one of those fabled wish generators. After all, I had been honing and refining the perfect wish for thirty years. "I wish for a million tax-free dollars that result from my own merit without any death or inheritance involved and do not involve any physical distress or disability or loss of anything in return."

I was pretty proud of that wish. I thought I had managed to hit every potential trip-wire and circumvent it. I wasn't trying to hurt anyone else with the wish; I stipulated that I had earned the payout; I should be physically able to enjoy the windfall. It seemed perfect to me.

It wasn't, of course, or you wouldn't be here listening to my tale of woe. It's that phrase "my own merit." That's rather vague, isn't it? I *should* have said something like "that result from the writing of a bestselling novel" or "that result from a record deal" or something else talent-based. Well, I guess this *is* talent-based. Just not the talent I had in mind.

I know you can't comment—but I have become pretty good at mind-reading over the years. I know what you're thinking. "What an idiot."

Yeah. I am. But I've also earned that million dollars a dozen times since I met that weird little man in the alley who offered to make my wish

124

come true if I reciprocated by granting his own desire.

He handed me this gun and this dagger and said, "I've heard good things about you." Who could resist following someone like that anywhere? Like I say, it was a monkey's paw moment...

Don't worry. I'll make this quick. Part of your wife's wish was that I prolong the agony. She'll see how that works for her when I go back to finish off the job. Can't leave any loose ends, can I?

You know what they say about wishes...

Aunt Maizie (LaVern Spencer McCarthy)

School was out for the summer and Williard and his twin brother, Dilliard, were happy. They couldn't wait to spend their days sleeping late, exploring the woods near their home and catching fish in the river. They wanted to see their friends and also go to the circus coming to town in a week or two.

Unfortunately, Mom and Dad had other ideas. They had booked reservations to attend a nudist camp for two weeks and of course the boys could not go. It would strain their sensitivities. Grandma, who lived with them, was not welcome to go either. She would have a hissy fit if she even knew what they were up to.

The boys were checking their fishing lures when Dad popped into their room.

"Hey, boys," he said. "Your mother and I are going on a two week vacation. We.ve made arrangements for you two and your Grandma to visit Aunt Maizie in Harbunkle, Kansas." Dillard threw his lure back into the tackle box.

"We don't want to go," he whined. Grandma, who sat on the bed, looked at her son sternly.

"You know good and well that Maizie is no good. I wouldn't let her be around my pet pig if I had one. She is my daughter, but she is evil!" Dad looked at her fondly. He walked over and patted her back.

"Just because she had that run-in with the law once when she hog-tied the sheriff and left him in the middle of Main Street doesn't mean she's all bad."

"Humph," went Grandma. "I wouldn't put anything past that woman. The last time I heard anything about her, she was into the occult." Dad gave her his sternest expression.

"You have to go anyway. We can't trust you to be here with the boys by yourself. I know Dillard and Willard are almost sixteen, but you're too unstable to be left here without supervision."

Grandma glared at him. "If you're talking about when I set my bedroom on fire, that was over five years ago," she sniffed.

"But you never stopped smoking," Dad reminded her.

"I only smoke two a day," she grumbled.

"Two packs a day," Dad replied. "Not only are you going with the boys to visit Maizie, you are going to have to do without cigarettes during that time. Maizie doesn't allow smoking in her house."

"Well, whoop-ti-do," Grandma sneered. "You have everything planned out, don't you? Where are you two going anyway" Dad's face turned red.

"None of your business." Grandma looked at him knowingly.

"I'll bet you are going to that nudist camp in Dodge City," I've seen brochures about it all over the house."

"That's not true," Dad lied. He retrieved three round trip bus tickets from his pocket.

"Here," he said, giving one to each person. "You leave in three days. Have your bags packed and ready to go." Grandma looked sadly at the boys.

"Well, you're going to have to put up with me for a while whether you like it or not." Dillard ran to his grandma to hug her.

"We don't mind," he assured her. "We love to be around you."

"Yeah!" seconded Williard. "We'll have a real good time." Grandma wasn't so sure, but she didn't want to discourage the boys before they started.

Three days later they were on their way to Harbunkle to see Maizie. Grandma kept bumming cigarettes from the people riding the bus until Williard gave her part of his newspaper money to buy them.

They had only one suitcase for the three of them. Each boy had a couple of shirts and trousers and several pairs of underwear and socks. Williard also carried three sleeping bags in a large, heavy-duty canvas bag.. Grandma only taken had a few items to wear since she knew this was not to be an extended visit. She kept the return bus tickets in her purse, ready to be used as soon as possible.

She had no desire to spend time with her Maizie. There had been too many incidents in the past for Grandma to trust her. However, she would try to make the best of the visit. Perhaps she and the boys could stay gone a lot for two weeks.

The three walked from the bus station to Aunt Maizie's house. It was in a derelict part of town. Strangers stared as they passed by. One guy who looked like a gangster snickered and said something about ugly, old Grandma. Grandma ran up to him and kicked him in the shin. He limped away whimpering.

"You're not as tough as you thought, huh, boy?" she shouted after him. They reached Aunt Maizie's house and were appalled by the sight of it. Tall weeds grew in the yard. The house needed paint and the shutters hung by a nail or two. The area around the place smelled like a backed-up sewer. Grandma and the boys pushed through the weeds and approached the residence warily.

When Aunt Maizie answered the doorbell, she looked as if she had been on a two week drunken spree. Her eyes widened at the sight of them.

"I thought you would be here next week," she told them." I haven't got much to eat at the moment.

"Don't worry about it," Grandma answered as she pushed her way past her daughter. She looked around the living room. There were cobwebs with dead bugs in them everywhere.

"Where's the broom?" Grandma asked Maizie. "I'll help tidy up this wretched place. Those cobwebs have got to go."

"No!" Maizie shouted. "Those are my snacks!" Grandma turned to look at her, aghast.

"Since when did you start eating dead bugs?"

"Since I learned they're a good source of protein," Maizie told her. Williard and Dillard snickered.

"Grandma, I heard she was off her rocker and now I know for sure," Willard said. Maizie rounded on him.

"Shut up, you little jerk!" she screeched. "I'll eat whatever I please."

Grandma frowned. "And what exactly are *we* supposed to eat while we are here?"

"I don't care if you starve!" Maizie snarled.

Grandma and the boys went to the nearest McDonalds for dinner. Grandma could not believe how much Maizie had changed in the several years since she had seen her.

She had developed long, spindly legs and arms. Her torso was oval shaped. She was nearly bald, only a few sparse hairs grew around her ears. She wore a black dress with a bright red symbol of some kind on the bodice. Her feet were clad in red heels and she wore red framed glasses. Grandma couldn't put her finger on what had changed, but Maizie looked odd.

Since Maizie did not own a television or computer, the boys were extremely bored. Grandma was not, but she was curious.

"What do you do around here and how are you surviving?"

Maizie glared at her. "None of your business!" she spat.

"Okay, okay," Grandma replied. "There's no reason for you to be so hateful."

"There's an arcade half a mile from here," Maizie informed her mother. "You and the boys' hair."

"What hair?" inquired Dillard, then burst into howls of laughter.

"Humph," said Grandma. "I can see we are not wanted around here." She grabbed her purse. "Come on, boys, let's go."

The boys loved going to an arcade, no argument there. After getting directions from Maizie, they were on their way.

"I wonder why Aunt Maizie is so gripey?" Williard said.

"I don't know," replied Grandma, avoiding a broken place in the sidewalk. "We may have to shorten our visit even if your parents don't want us to."

"We will if we have to," Dillard assured her. "We trust you, Grandma. You have never let us down."

Grandma smiled. "And I won't," she told him. "I can watch after you two at home as well as here."

After several hours at the arcade the trio had sandwiches and drinks at the arcade snack bar. They decided to go back to Maizie's house for the night, but all three were leery. Grandma said she had bad vibes but would try to make the best of it.

There was no one at Maizie's home,. They looked through the filthy house, calling for her. They wondered if she had gone out for the evening, so they put their sleeping bags in the middle of the living room floor and crawled in.

In the middle of the night Williard jerked awake. He felt as though something was choking him. He grabbed his neck. It felt hot and painful. Had something bitten him? He whispered to Dilliard,

"Are you awake?"

"Yes," came the reply. "Something bit me."

"Me too," said Williard.

"Here, also," Grandma whispered. "Everything is black." No streetlights illuminated the living room as before.

"Where are we?" Dilliard asked.

"I don't know," admitted Williard. "Something is very strange." He felt around. His hand touched

131

something soft like cotton candy or spun cotton. He tried to move the substance. It was strong. Grandma's foot touched his knee. They were close to each other. Williard touched Dilliard's shoulder. They were wrapped in something that felt sinister. Some sort of slime covered them completely. They soon realised they were trapped inside a cocoon-like structure. Williard cut a small hole in the substance with his pocket knife and peered through it.

"What do you see?" Grandma whispered. Williard could not believe what he was looking at.

"It's a spider."

"What's it doing?"

"It's sitting at a table reading a newspaper."

"This is no time for jokes!" Grandma hissed.

"It's no joke," Williard said. "It looks like a big black widow spider with several pairs of red plastic framed monocles and red stiletto heels on five of its feet. Two other legs are holding the newspaper and one leg has a cup of tea the spider is sipping. It has a red hour glass on its stomach. I think it's Aunt Maizie."

Grandma nudged Williard away from the hole and peered through it.

"I remember a birthmark she had on her head. I can still see an outline of it," Grandma whispered. Williard shuddered.

"What do you think she plans to do with us?" he asked Grandma. Grandma turned away from the hole and let Dilliard have a peek.

"She plans to eat us, most likely," she told him. Dilliard moved away from the hole.

"We can't let that happen," he decided. "We will have to trick her somehow."

132

"Yeah, we have to get out of here," Williard agreed. "For now let's try to rest." From their position in relation to the table Maizie-Spider sat at, Williard knew they must be hanging on the wall.

The cocoon was huge. It held the three of them, their sleeping bags and the canvas bag they had used to haul them in. Grandma had her purse with her by some miracle. The three of them had vicious headaches from being drugged with some form of venom. Fortunately, no real harm had come to them, yet.

They slept on top of their sleeping bags because the cocoon was stuffy from lack of ventilation. While they slept, the hole Williard had made was being widened. Around two o'clock in the morning Dilliard felt something brush his face. He was awake instantly. He sat up. Several red eyes were watching him. He screamed.

Grandma and Williard jerked awake. They screamed also, not knowing what was happening but afraid. Dry, creepy, feathery spider legs were all over them as the spider made her way into the cocoon.

"Kick it!" Dilliard shrieked. They did, but it took several attempts before they were able to force it out of the cocoon. Finally, it hissed and withdrew.

"It bit me!" Dilliard whimpered. There was no sleep for anyone the rest of the night. When morning finally arrived, the three tried to think of a way to escape.

"Try to cut another hole with your knife," Dilliard suggested. Williard began to explore their prison with his knife. He struck something solid. After much effort, he felt the outer wall their prison

133

was attached to, crumble, making a hole big enough for escape. He was relieved that the walls were rotten.

"If we escape, she will come after us," Grandma said. "We have to trap her." The boys agreed, but how? They decided to wait for nightfall to trap the spider. All three were very hungry and thirsty but had nothing to eat or drink.

"When we get out of this, I will buy us Big Macs and huge colas," Williard promised.

"Yes, and I'm going to give my son and your mother a piece of my mind," Grandma said.

"I know they went to that nasty nudist camp even though they denied they were going there." The boys snorted.

"We knew all the time," Dillard confessed. "I heard them talking about it when they thought they were alone."

That night around 11: 00 they laid their trap. They told Grandma to crawl out of the hole Williard had made and wait for them nearby, which she did. Around 2:00 a.m they heard the spider as she began to widen the hole she had closed when she left the cocoon the first time.

"Shh", Willard whispered. "It won't be long now." *Come on, come on, you piece of evil*. The boys waited until they could tell she was fully inside the cocoon.

"Now!" shouted Williard. "Pull the strings tight!" They heard a squeal as they closed the top of the canvas bag they had brought from home. It was very heavy and strong. They had placed the top of it at the entrance of the hole the spider had made. She crawled into it. She would not be able to chew her way out of it even if she turned back into a human and she would die. It was lucky that Maizie-Spider had enclosed it in the cocoon she had trapped them in. Hopefully she would suffocate soon.

The twins hurriedly escaped their prison and were on their way to the bus station. Grandma had no idea how her daughter had changed into a spider, but she was glad to be leaving that horrible place. They had to wait for the next available bus, but were soon on their way home. They had a circus to attend and lots of fishing to do.

Peas In A Pod (Victoria Nangle)

What scares me? This scares me. Waking early with the sure-fire knowledge that somebody I love, somebody I cherish, somebody who has been an intrinsic part of my life for the last 30 years – that specific somebody is going to be cut into today.

Regardless of whatever happens today, you will be woven into my life forever. Because you don't just stop having someone to love and care for, and need to speak to in times of trouble, or just for a giggle – because they're not there. You will always be in my heart, like a piece of shrapnel from a war we both lived through that keeps on burning around us. We have each other's backs in this skirmish, or that lull in the action. We have laughed the dark humour of troubles. And we have flown high with dangerous carefree abandon, when all felt rosy and like nothing would dare go against us.

And there will be more. This knife will not stop us. It will not cut us. Except that it will cut you. This is what scares me. And it terrifies you.

Selfishly, I cannot lose you. And I will not. Ever. Any more than you could ever lose me. We are woven like a dreadlock together – unfathomable to anyone who would seek to untangle us. No one can, and don't you even look to think that you could try! I will fight you with the fury of a tiger if you even think about it.

I've never cried with fear before. I suppose I must have when I was younger and scared myself halfway up a mountain, trapping myself with a bad cliff hold and needing help. Or thought I'd lost my mum in the market back when everyone else was a sea of legs. I can't do a thing about this fear. But message you. You've just messaged me...

Our words... it's like the last few months have served as pencil sharpeners for our words as we left more and more precise marks for each other in WhatsApp, like soft lead leaving it's graphite mark – like a vapour trail from an aeroplane that just won't stop going forward towards today. I'm treasuring these exchanges so much. You shine so bright. It's peculiar, the weaker your body became the stronger your words delivered – chosen with a specific care. Even the careless words between us fell to capture us at our most conspiratorial, like kids having a midnight feast in a blanket fort.

I've lit a candle. It's rose geranium scented. I don't light candles. Other people say they'll light a candle for me or a troubled friend when we talk sometimes. I don't light candles for people, I light them for mood lighting. I've lit a candle as if every bit of warmth and light makes a difference for you. Maybe it does. I chose one with a scent and brand that I think that you wouldn't be ashamed to have in your own home. Less your common bog-standard Wee Willy Winkie candlestick, more of a nice smelly. And I did it for you. Come home. Please.

We still have conversations to be held about people who smell funny – and whether we smell funny! About what toenails are really for. About the power of linguistics and the etymology of language. Reassurance before a dental appointment, tell me the shirt size of my godson, remote watching of

RuPaul's Drag Race as we text our costume-'Oooh's and backchat-'ahhhhh's.

I'm not crying anymore, I'm looking at our last few text message exchanges. I've printed them all out from the last few months into a booklet, and popped one of those wee dolls we made at uni into a jiffy bag with it. To send to you on the Other Side of this. We are goddamn formidable. And nothing is ever going to change that. No goddamn knife. No goddamn cancer. We are powerful, even as others take our power. We have words, and when they are gone we have attitude. We have a self-belief that if it ever dares to shimmer comes back at full blaze through the eyes of the other. And regardless of whatever life throws at us, we will always be able to see ourselves through the other's eyes. To have that perspective is a gift – it's a miracle! - and we've found it.

We are so blessed that perhaps the world had to throw some shit at us just to stop the rest of them from killing us in green-eyed envy. I love you. And I know that you love me. Always and forever. Through sulks and partners, strops and distance. Nothing stops this love.

You message me that you're scared. I guide you, I distract you – it's what I do. You are loved, you are held, can you remember the number of steps there are in your house? – count them now. I shall take your mind away from where it is. Remember the feel of the deep carpet beneath your feet, you are practically incapable of living with anything but the softest pillows, mattress, duvet, carpet – anything around you that could be plush, is. Remember your sofa, in all its deep velvety goodness, so deep I have

138

struggled to get out of it on occasion. I tell you this and I know that a small part of your head is laughing at the mental image of my flailing limbs, even as you are being wheeled on that hard gurney down the flat white hallways, with harsh lights overhead flashing by.

You text that you are going into theatre now and that your sister will message me when you get out. Think of me, I message. Think of me, focus on me, feel the energy and devotion I am sending, let it hold you like a marionette's strings when you have no muscle mass of your own. Let me hold you. Focus on me, and let that keep you safe. It will!

I am willing all of the love in my head and body, every single little bit, drawing it up with all of my fear and every bit of my fury, from my toenails and fingertips, the very surface of my skin – see the hairs on my arms stand out straight as if I was an angry cat! Shooting this concentrated fierce love out mentally from the middle of my forehead, like a laser beam to you.

To a casual glance I probably look constipated. I'm the very opposite. Figuratively speaking. Are you laughing inside again?

I've paper-cut my finger on the pages I'm writing upon as I turn to a fresh sheet. My scrawl has gotten big and greedy – you know my handwriting.

I watch the small amount of blood pool within my fingerprint. Captivated. Almost hypnotised. Your blood must look so much like my blood. I wonder if our haemoglobin is coming to the surface at the same time. We're still connected – I know you must feel it. Don't for a moment think that distraction means interruption. Don't let the powers of the universe thank that. I won't bear it. To double down on our connection I squeeze the crest of my fingertip with the cut on it over the candle flame, and watch it flare with the alien red drop's intervention – once, twice, three times.

I reach for another of our uni dolls – I hung on to loads of them. Don't you find they just turn up? We used to come back half cut from a student weekend club night of sticky floors and equally self-delusional undergraduate chat-up lines. We'd stumble in for a debrief in the kitchen, giggling, with a latex glove each we'd grabbed from the box at the end of the catering bar – the only things we could reach through the metal cage shutters that barred the plundering of student midnight snacks.

And then – remember how we thought we were so clever and creative with this? We draw faces on the plastic fingertips in biro and cast our little men as players, in our wish fulfilment as to how the evenings should've gone. Like Barbies on alcopops.

Then we'd both raid our hairbrushes and stuff the things with shed knots of bottle blonde strands and hennaed brunette locks, before sellotaping the puppet doll things shut.

I know exactly what I'm doing.

I cut the aged doll open.

Scatter the dry dead hair into the candle flame – the sharp edges catch the heat instantly and fly off on an updraft from the open window – I'm chasing the fire-bugged remnants around the room! Can you see me from your anaesthetised dream state? I'm flapping on random air draughts! Frantically batting at sizzles threatening to ignite my library of long collected high and low literature. Can you see? I tap out my sixth form Collected Chaucer, where the dust is proving alarmingly flammable. An orange flicker elsewhere has me run to Percy Jackson & The Lightning Thief, slap it with the side of my palm into extinction.

My notes – these notes! The smell of scorched paper is filling my nostrils, but not half as much as burnt old hair.

I feel a bit lightheaded by the whole endeavour and a part of my addled brain imagines that your agitated spirit flew in through the open window and threw the whole shebang around the study in a wild release of frustration. I wouldn't blame you if you had.

There are small, charred marks on the paper, and I feel a twisted satisfaction that there is proof that I almost set myself alight while you are under the knife.

The candle is burning, the flame jumping around in tethered excitement, snapping sparks. I look to see what is sparking and it's hair. And blood. They're doing a thing. Together. It's fascinating and weird. I can't describe... My vision keeps sliding off it, like trying to catch mercury with my eyes...

My chest hurts.

I miss you so much.

I can't stand the patience I need to get through to the other side, to wait for your sister to message your groggy dictation. I need your groggy dictation.

The sparks have gone – conquered or self-extinguished. The no-longer-alight room's smells here are changing. The fiery-ness is dying down and

141

the Autumn is blowing in. But it doesn't smell of soggy leaves and bonfires. Not even of rose and geranium candle wax. I'm opening up my nose to try and identify what I can smell for you, sniffing the air – please wake up and be alright – I'm begging. I'll get down on my knees to the Powers That Be.

Someone must be washing their car or something outside, I think I can smell Fairy liquid – or maybe Domestos – who's cleaning their car with bleach?! It could be those students across the road – do you think they overindulged last night and cleaned up the mess this morning? - it's coming through strong though, och – we were never that bad, I'm sure. We'll paint the town red next time though, you and me?

No, it's not bleach – it keeps changing – it's antiseptic. Yes, with hints of soap – it's quite overwhelming, I'm going to have to sit down and put my head between my knees.

How are you feeling? Please wake up. I feel rotten. My chest is still hurting and my head feels woozy. I'd close the window if I could get up. And that smell! I'm lying low with my eyes almost closed and there's, like, an electric light that keeps coming to the back of my eyelids – flip, flip, flipping like a strobe lightning loop. There's not even any kind of electric lighting on in this room. Sorry, I really shouldn't mutter about me when you're going through so much. But I do feel wretched. It's come on so strong… I'll put my head down here… it's so heavy… sorry… I love you… I can't- …

"SHE'S AWAKE."

A Place The Night Can't Touch (Paul Edwards)

I. Together Alone

Choice excerpts from the diary of Francine Russo, 17 years old:

Oct 2nd

Marvin has ripped chunks out of my favourite dress. I suppose it's my fault really; I shouldn't have left it hanging around, although I make a point of not speaking to him for the rest of the day.

Oct 3rd

Spent all day running around the house, making sure the slats are nice and firm across the windows and doors. Just noticed there's a dead dog out in the garden; it's been ripped apart and half-eaten by the Creeps, its exposed innards looking like pink, wet snakes in the grass.

Oct 5th

Drove into town earlier to ransack the grocery store for food, but the shop stank and the shelves were pretty much empty. Then I got home to discover Marvin had been in my bedroom. He's ripped my beautiful, leather-bound Hans Christian

Anderson book of fairy tales to shreds and eaten most of the pages.

I feel so angry and depressed, and I'm seriously thinking about muzzling him again.

Oct 6th

I've concluded that muzzling Martin wouldn't do *any* good at all – it would be an enormous step backwards. I have to condition him not to do these things; in the same way I conditioned him not to eat me!

When rooting through the kitchen cabinets this afternoon, I found a small tin of red paint. An idea formed in my mind which might help bring Marvin to heel at last...

Oct 16th

Last night I forgot to put my earplugs in and woke to the sound of the Creeps scratching and clawing at my front door.

I sat up straight, listening to their thwarted groans. One of them bashed its head repeatedly against the door in a desperate bid to get in. I leaned across and lit the blood-red candle beside my bed, crimson light wavering across the walls.

"You'll *never* get in," I hissed. "I'm safe here. Nothing can touch me!"

I snatched up my earplugs, then put them in and blew out the candle.

Darkness and silence reigned.

Oct 29th

a.m. Training is complete – I hope! I shall conduct a little experiment this afternoon to see if all my hard work has paid off.

p.m. I waited patiently in the kitchen, where everything was carefully prepared. Marvin – hungry, searching for food – finally appeared, his giant shadow falling across the wall. He looked around with sunken eyes, seeing the remnants of last night's meal on the table – warmed up beans and mash. He gazed at it, sniffed, and for a horrible moment I was sure he was going to eat it. Then he turned his head and stared at the open tin of dog food on the counter.

"Go on," I gestured to the tin with an excited nod of my head.

Marvin looked at me.

"Go on, boy."

He made his way over to the counter, moaning, grunting incomprehensibly. He stared at the red paint daubed on the raised lid of the tin and I bit my nails in anticipation. Then he spooned his fingers into the tin and patted the processed meat into his mouth and I emitted an insuppressible shriek of delight.

"Well done!" I said, clapping my hands. "Good boy! *Good* boy!"

Nov 3rd

The paint is working a treat, although somehow I managed to get some on the kitchen cabinet door, don't ask me how. I walked into the room to find

145

Marvin with his mouth clamped around the edge of the cabinet, trying to eat the thing! I couldn't help myself – I dissolved into tears of laughter. Then there was a *snap* and the wood splintered and a couple of molars tumbled out of Marvin's mouth.

"Oh dear!" I cried, grabbing the kitchen roll from the cupboard. "Let's clean you up."

He's sitting in the lounge now feeling sorry for himself, God bless his soul.

Nov 4th

I've retired to my room, leaving Marvin alone in the lounge. He's sat on his stool, eyes fixed on nothing in particular on the wall.

I gaze out my bedroom window at the nightscape beyond. The moon stares back like a sunken eyeball, its light blanketing the pot plants and two cars in the driveway below. The blue Escort doesn't start up anymore and the yellow Citroen is almost out of fuel; soon I might not be able to make my weekly run into town for food.

Earlier I saw the Creeps loitering by the woods. Perhaps I was being paranoid, but I swear they were looking straight back at me...

Nov 7th

I was reading an old Anne McCaffrey novel in the lounge when I looked up and tried guessing at what Marvin's actual name might be. I only call him Marvin because he kind of looks like a Marvin.

"You okay?" I asked.

His head swivelled round, a big ugly smile cracking across his face.

He may be stupid and slow, but he's nothing like the Creeps outside. Not now, anyway. And I feel so comfortable around him.

He's the closest thing I have to a friend.

II. An Intrusion

Nov 13th

a.m. I left Marvin to his own devices and spent time watching the world through my bedroom window.

In the distance the Creeps were gathering by the fencing segregating the woods from the garden. I watched them stumble and fall into each other like drunkards.

Suddenly a woman emerged from the woods, slipping in the mud and rain, bleeding from cuts to her arms and legs. She glanced around with wide, frightened eyes, then focused her gaze on the house.

I shrank away from the window.

"My God," I whispered. "This can't be real."

I looked again.

She climbed clumsily over the fence, ran the length of the drive and tried the doors to both the Escort and Citroen. Then she charged toward the house, her long dark hair whipping about her face, her pale arms swinging by her sides. She reached the door and pounded with her fists. "Please," she screamed, "let me in! Somebody – *let me in!*"

I felt sick and confused.

The Creeps poured forward, staggering with their arms outstretched toward her.

"PLEASE! For God's sake, if there's anybody in there – LET ME IN!"

There wasn't any more time to think – I ran downstairs, lifted the slats and released the catches to the front door. The woman squeezed her way in, a maggoty face hovering and groaning in the gap she'd left behind.

I slammed the door.

Silence.

She fell back against the wall, her long, wet hair dangling in front of her face. "Thank you," she said. "*Thank* you."

I glanced at Marvin sitting in the shadows of the lounge and before she could look, I closed the door on him.

"You... okay?" I asked.

She flung her skinny arms around me and began to cry – huge, choked sobs of relief. I felt her trembling against me and I was so scared because I knew I'd done the wrong thing.

p.m. "I'm so glad I found you," she said, her eyes black-ringed, her face furrowed and drawn. "My name's Helen. I was living in town when..." She folded her arms across her chest, puffed out her cheeks and looked away.

I stared at the floor, not knowing what to say.

"What's your name?" she asked, turning to me again.

"Fran."

She smiled. "I haven't seen anyone alive in weeks. I've been hiding away in the cellar beneath

148

my house. One night those things broke in and almost caught me... but I escaped." She fingered a silver St. Christopher around her neck.

"What do you think happened?" she asked at last. "I mean... is this some form of punishment, you know, from God? Or a science experiment gone wrong?"

I stared at my hands, as though searching for her answer in the creases and folds of my skin.

"My husband, Harry... h-he died suddenly six months ago. A heart defect, see. But then when I saw him that morning, standing in the porch... it was as if all my nightmares had turned *real*." Her eyes welled with tears. "He tried to kill me. God... *He tried to eat me*."

I began putting those items daubed in red paint away into cupboards and drawers. Helen watched on, confusion spread across her features. "Hey," I said, turning quickly. "Why don't you go rest? You look *so* tired. There's a spare bedroom upstairs; first door on the left."

"Yes," she said, nodding. "Yes, thanks Fran. I think I will."

She hesitated on her way out. "Is this your house?"

"No." I shook my head. "Don't know who it belonged to."

"Wasn't there anybody here?"

I thought of Marvin.

He was here.

I found him locked in the attic, just after I'd boarded up the house.

"No," I said. "Nobody."

Helen smiled. "We're going to be okay here, aren't we? We can get through this, now that we've found each other."

"Yes," I said, returning the smile. But it was a strained smile, a false smile; it didn't reflect how utterly detached I was feeling from the world.

An hour later I crept upstairs carrying the pot of red paint. I grabbed my earplugs from off the top of the bedside cabinet and slipped them into my pocket. Then I crossed the hall and tapped gently on the spare bedroom door. No reply. I opened it and found Helen fast asleep, her hair splashed out across the pillows.

I moved to the foot of the bed. "Sorry," I said, the word hanging in the air around me.

You must understand, it's not that I didn't like Helen. It's just I liked my world the way it was; everything was so simple and without complications. You see, the house, this place, it's all mine, it belongs to me. It's my own private, secret world and nothing can touch it – not the night, not anyone.

I leaned over Helen and her eyelashes fluttered. I dipped my finger into the tin of paint and touched her forehead. She didn't stir.

Marvin was searching the kitchen for food when I came back downstairs.

"Marvin," I said, pointing to the ceiling. "Try up there. *Up* there." He turned his head and looked at me. He can't read guilt or fear and that's what I love so much about him – he can't detect any weakness in me at all. "Upstairs," I said again.

He nodded and moaned excitedly and I thought I caught a glimmer of understanding in those black, black eyes.

He lurched past me and climbed the stairs and as I heard him enter the spare bedroom, I pushed the plugs into my ears so I wouldn't hear a thing.

That's Your Funeral (Carl Hughes)

Steve steered his big Mercedes through the night. *Thrust* it through the night, he thought, relishing a word that packed as much ruthlessness as himself.

He was used to the blast of heavy metal from his car's hi-fi and revelled in the magic from being on the move while most people slept. These pre-dawn hours belonged to him alone and he felt them vibrating in his bones. He liked working in the hours after midnight.

In this earliest part of Monday he was returning from another mission undertaken for Bertie Mann, casino owner and bookmaker. Five years as an enforcer for Bertie had taught Steve all about the enjoyable side of brutality. His job involved calling on those casino and turf clients who either couldn't or wouldn't pay up. Bigshots, some of them, or at least they thought so. In daily life they bullied their secretaries, demolished egos and trod on the weak. But when Steve came calling, they changed. Oh yes indeed. Steve ensured they paid their debts to Bertie – or else. It was the "or else" that he liked best. Tonight, for instance, he'd left one quivering wreck of a punter with a busted nose and several smashed ribs.

Steve guessed the jerk would get twenty grand or so together somehow as these mugs usually did. If not, there'd be another visit.

The Merc hurtled around a succession of bends on the Cheshire lane, disturbing a ghostly owl as it tore into prey on the verge. Then, in the midst of Steve's wandering thoughts and tuneless humming, a maniac driver came slewing around a tight bend, half on the wrong side of the road, heading towards him at bullet speed.

Steve was dazzled by headlights, yelled a curse and swung hard left. His door mirror exploded as it met that of the other car. The Merc bucked and bit into a wildflower verge before shredding a hedge like confetti and hurtling towards a belt of trees. For a crazy second it seemed to Steve that one of the trees had become mobile. It reeled towards him, weaving this way and that, determined to block his path. Mercedes and tree met in a thumping embrace.

Steve felt in an instant as if a length of the most mighty elastic was ripping him through space. No tunnel or white light – the sort of crap he'd read about – only a kaleidoscope of fragments like pixels disintegrating on a computer screen.

The experience lasted for a handful of seconds. Then he found himself in the living room of his home, near the ceiling in a corner by the window. It seemed to him that only a few heartbeats had passed since he crashed the Merc but it must have been much longer, daylight had arrived. Indeed, sunshine flooded through the mesh curtains, strobing like celestial bars around the twenty or so people gathered there. Among them were Steve's family, his gym pals and a few colleagues from Bertie Mann's payroll. All wore black. Not head-to-foot mourning but black somewhere, from the men's ties to the women's skirts and jackets. Flowers also proliferated and fragrance like a florist's shop. It was then that he noticed the coffin.

"Jesus!" he gasped. The box stood on a purple-draped bier against the wall where normally he'd find the display cabinet containing his karate and boxing trophies. From his elevated position he could see the coffin's occupant. Himself, of course. In his dinner jacket. But Steve didn't *feel* dead. A catastrophic mistake was clearly being played out.

Above a muted babble of voices he called, "Some idiot's cocked up. I'm still alive."

No one took any notice. They went on talking among themselves. A few even laughed, showing no respect for the apparently dead. Their callousness angered Steve, but what troubled him most was their inability to see or hear him. He found that scary and fear to him was an alien emotion.

Cilla sat across the room on a tan-leather Chesterfield talking to divorced neighbour Jason Bartram. Cilla didn't look much like a grieving widow despite the obligatory black. In fact she had a bloom about the cheeks that Steve hadn't seen for years. He hurried towards her, finding that the desire to move was sufficient to propel him. He floated across the space, descending as he went.

"Cilla, what the hell's going on?" he demanded.

Cilla didn't pause in her prattle. "So I intend to get rid of Steve's fricking awful games room and use it as another conservatory," she was saying to Bartram.

"Yeah, a conservatory with a wide, deep divan where we can screw the afternoons away," Bartram smiled. "I'm getting a hard on just thinking about it."

154

Cilla giggled, prodding him. "Down, boy," she said. "Remember this is supposed to be a sad occasion."

"Sure – bring out the bunting," Bartram chortled.

Steve gaped. How long had this been going on? A deep stillness settled over him. It was dangerous, that stillness – anyone who'd ever run up against him could testify to that. From this moment he wouldn't be satisfied until he'd turned Bartram into dead meat. And Cilla, he'd knock crap out of the cheating bitch and kick her into the street. Yes, he'd do it as soon as he got this mix-up sorted.

He flung a glance across the room to another sofa on which his son and daughter sat with sour faces. At least they weren't laughing, unlike some others. He rushed across to them.

"Daniel, Kerry," he said, "tell them your dad's alive."

For a second, as her eyes seemed to fasten on his, he thought Kerry could see him. Then she sighed and said to her brother, "Really boring, this is. Trust Dad to mess up my weekend. He knew I wanted to go camping with the Rangers."

"He didn't wrap his car around that tree just to spite you," Daniel said. "But I know what you mean. I don't see why we have to be here. What's the point? There's nothing we can do except pretend to look sad." He glanced at his watch. "I wish the undertaker'd hurry up so we can get this thing over."

"Then return to normal," Kerry said.

155

"You heartless little toads!" Steve yelled. "Is this what I get for being a good father, seeing you want for nothing?"

The pair gazed through him, fretful and sullen.

Only then did Steve realise what Daniel had said about the undertaker. This wasn't several hours after the crash. It must be *days*. In fact, this must be his funeral. He hadn't twigged that before. These people weren't there simply to condole but to send him on his final journey. That stunned him. He gaped towards the casket.

A grizzled bull of a man sauntered by, glass of port like blood in one hand and cigar in the other. "So I'm putting pressure on the committee chairman," Bertie Mann was saying to his sidekick Terence Maguire, a weaselish entity whom Steve despised. "I've told him he'd better wangle me permission to expand or information about his sexual proclivities might get out."

Maguire sniggered. "No choice then, has he?"

"None," Bertie agreed. "But of course I sweetened it by promising a bung. That way he can pretend he's a bigtime player instead of a blackmailed dupe."

Steve stared at their departing backs. Not mourning the loss of their number one enforcer, were they? They stopped by the coffin for a moment, glanced at his body and moved on, still talking business.

"You bastards," Steve muttered.

Bitter, angry and fearful, he drifted across to the bier. His face in the coffin looked serene apart from a bash on the nose and lump on the forehead. Around his neck someone had placed his favourite

156

chain, the chunky gold one with diamond inserts: the one that Cilla called cheap and trashy. His hands were clasped, wedding ring reflecting the sunlight.

He reached out, wanting to know if he could touch his body. He couldn't. His etheric hand passed through the real ones. Yet the act must have caused something fundamental to happen because almost instantly he could feel the shirt cuffs around his wrists, the chill in his fingers, the hard pillow beneath his head. Surely that must mean some consciousness had slipped into the shell of flesh and bone. So why wasn't the rest of him there? Steve could only guess that the supernatural elastic hadn't done its job properly: it should have pulled him into his body but hadn't succeeded.

"Maybe if I try to climb inside," he murmured, knowing no one but he could hear the words. But then only he *needed* to hear them. He sought the reassurance of their sound.

Being disembodied spared him the indignity of having to clamber on to the bier and into his casket. He only had to think the actions and he rose and descended like a dandelion seed on a puff of air. He couldn't see his incorporeal body but sensed it drifting down on to its physical counterpart, head on head, arms on arms, feet on feet.

"Right then," he muttered. "Now I open my eyes."

He knew his eyes hadn't opened. Where that knowledge came from it wasn't possible to be sure, as at this point he lay both physically and spiritually inside his coffin and the spiritual part had been able to see all along. But he knew. He could still feel the shirt cuffs, the jacket, the pillow. Now he also experienced a slight tingling of pins and needles in his fingers as blood circulated with dire sluggishness. At least he could feel something, even if he couldn't yet open his eyes.

Okay, concentrate, he thought. *Focus your mind. Now then – sit up and scare the shit out of them all.*

He sat up. That is, the spiritual part of him sat up. The other bit, the business bit in the box, remained recumbent.

Bollocks! he thought. *So what happens now?*

Bertie Mann and the weasel had paused to exchange a word or two with Cilla and she looked suitably grief-stricken. Bertie stooped to kiss her cheek and moved on. No doubt he and the weasel had urged her to bear up and assured her what a great guy Steve had been. Now Bertie was helping himself to more port and probably talking business again. Other people sat or stood about gossiping. Someone laughed loudly and turned it into a cough.

"What a shower you are!" Steve bawled. His words reverberated around the room but only on whatever plane it was he occupied. In the world inhabited by those unfeeling arseholes the sound had less effect than a dust mote.

The pins and needles sharpened and the starched cuffs on Steve's wrists began to irritate him. These were good signs. They meant a stronger return of feeling. Now if he could just move a finger or even let loose a good fart, that would get everyone's attention. He tried but nothing happened.

Frustrated, he left the coffin and drifted among the mourners. He shouted into their faces, willing them to notice him. The only reaction he received was from dotty Great-Aunt Alice, who claimed to be psychic. Along with everyone else in the family Steve had always scoffed at her but now he realised they'd done the old girl an injustice. She looked up as he approached the straight-backed chair on which she sat with legs wide apart. For a second she frowned, then her eyes widened.

"Can you see me, Alice?" Steve yelped with sudden hope. He crouched, placing his face so close to hers that he could smell her sour breath.

"Steven?" she said. "Is that you, Steven?" She didn't precisely focus on him. Her eyes flicked left and right.

"Yes, it's me," Steve cried. "I'm not dead. Tell them there's been a mistake."

"I can sense your presence," Alice murmured.

"Don't whisper it, for God's sake," Steve raged. "Shout it so every bugger'll know."

Whether Alice heard him he couldn't be sure, but anyway she called, "Steven's here."

A hush fell over the room, followed by several sniggers and glances of amusement.

"Yes, of course he is, Great-Aunt," Steve's cousin Lucy said. She appeared from among the throng. "That's why we've gathered today."

"No, I don't mean that way. I mean in spirit," Alice insisted. "I can feel his presence."

"Well, that's nice. I'm sure he's glad to see such a good turnout and all these lovely flowers. Now, the hearse'll be here any minute. Hadn't you better use the loo?"

"Yes, I think I should or I might wet myself again," Alice said.

Steve stormed at her. "Don't go for a pee, you senile maggot. Tell them I'm alive."

It was no use. Lucy helped Alice off the chair and led her at a shuffle across the room towards the downstairs cloakroom. Alice asked as they went, "Are there salmon sandwiches for the reception?"

"Salmon and ham," Lucy said.

"Wouldn't mind a bit of salmon now," Alice told her.

"There's no time," Lucy said. "But you can have some when we get back from the crematorium."

Crematorium!

Steve howled with a despair that no one could hear. They were going to burn him. Not knowing he could feel things just as they could, they were going to put him into an incinerator.

Inside the coffin, his heartbeat quickened and warmth suffused his fingers. He felt the satin lining of the coffin against his neck where the cushion didn't reach. Physical sensations were returning at a rush. Yet strive as he might, hurrying to the bier, he couldn't produce even the tiniest twitch. He stared heavenwards, alternately begging and cursing whatever deity who'd sent him back on faulty elastic and done nothing to sort out the mess.

"The hearse is here," someone said. Steve sensed a ripple of relief among those in the room. He stopped cursing. That was having no effect. He hovered over his body, commanding it to work.

Two black-suited men from the funeral parlour moved towards him, evidently intending to lower the coffin lid. As they did so, Steve felt and saw a tic develop in his right cheek. A movement that

160

would tell them he was still alive. His right eyelid began to twitch, too, and a film of sweat burst across his forehead. He cried in exultation. He was about to be saved at the death. *At the death!* That expression produced a shrill, hysterical and silent laugh.

Then he screamed not with mirth but horror as Cilla said something to the two men, distracting them. They closed the lid without glancing at his body – they'd turned to look at Cilla instead.

"You stupid *bitch!*" Steve screeched at his wife. "You stopped them seeing."

Even with screws in place the lid wasn't an especially good fit: tiny gaps showed around the perimeter. Which meant some air would get in so he wouldn't even be granted the mercy of suffocation.

Calm down, Steve, he told himself. *Concentrate. If your cheek and eyelid are twitching, it means you're getting some movement back. Try hard enough and you should be able to move your hands, rap on the lid.*

So he concentrated and felt his clasped fingers flutter, but his arms wouldn't obey the instruction to rise.

Don't panic, he urged, hyperventilating in whatever world he occupied. *There's time yet. The journey to the crematorium's bound to take ten minutes or more, then there's the service – at least another twenty minutes. Half an hour in all. You'll be jumping around like a new-born lamb by then.*

The thought encouraged him but didn't quell his horror.

161

As they carried the coffin outside he heard Great-Aunt Alice say, "I can feel Steven's presence. He's quite emotional."

Emotional, you silly cow? It should be you in this box, not me.

The cortège moved off, through the leafy estate and on to a main road past the shops where a few elderly men ducked their heads in tribute. Steve scarcely noticed. He went on sweating metaphysical blood trying to raise his hands. He felt the muscles tighten and even managed to shift his left elbow just as they reached the crematorium.

Mourners filed inside, sat in pews, a cleric whom he had never met said nice things about him, Bertie Mann stood up and did the same, and the cleric said, "We will now sing *The Lord's My Shepherd*."

They sang lustily. Too lustily. The din overwhelmed Steve's rapping. Well, a tapping really, just the feeblest snap with his fingernails on the coffin lid. Less noise than a mouse would make in the wainscot; but at least a genuine, audible Earth sound. Or it would be once those cretins stopped singing.

Trouble was, they didn't. They'd only just started on the third verse when a purple curtain began slowly to unfurl, eventually obscuring the coffin from their view. Yelling again, willing his fingers to bang rather than tap, Steve saw the mourners putting down their hymn books, getting up and shuffling out. The racket of their feet on the woodblock floor smothered any sound from the coffin. Despite his efforts, Steve's hands fell back as if sinking through a jar of jellied glue.

Steve had never considered what happened behind the scenes at a crematorium. Now, not wanting to know, he found out. Two middle-aged men and a dull youth slouched up to remove the coffin. They wore grubby jeans and sloppy, greasy T-shirts with sweat stains around the necks and beneath the arms. Incongruously, each had a plastic name tag pinned to his T-shirt as if he might meet a corpse that would demand some ID.

They dragged the coffin on to a gurney and wheeled it through a set of rubber swing doors. A stone-tiled corridor led to more swing doors which opened into the crematorium's real business area – a lofty, whitewashed chamber with concrete floor and harsh fluorescent lights. Steve stared at a line of six cremators set into the right-hand wall, their doors gaping. Five of the cremators already contained coffins.

"OK, Damon, now's your chance to show what you've learned this week," one of the men said, talking to the youth. Steve saw from the man's name tag that he was called George Parkinson.

"Maybe you should show me once more," the youth said. He looked nervy.

"God – it's simple enough, son," the second man said. Laurie Swetman, according to his tag. An appropriate surname for someone employed in this place.

"Yeah, but I'm still new and I don't like..." Damon licked his lips. "I mean, I didn't know you did this sort of thing."

The men grinned. "It's the only perk we get in our job," George said. "There's no productivity bonus here, you know."

Steve heard all this but barely took it in. In fact he wished the trio would shut up. He wanted to focus his mindpower, all his energy, on forcing his hands to move again. If he didn't rap on the lid within the next minute or so it would be too late.

Now, he told himself. *Do it now*. His right hand lifted and brushed the lid of the coffin but fell away again through the same glue as before. Steve raged and screamed, but only on the celestial plane where no one could hear. Inside the box, his body had become soaked with a sweat of panic. It trickled down his forehead, prickled along the neck of his shirt, even soaked into the satin that lined the coffin's sides. All these feelings, yet he couldn't summon the strength to let anyone know.

"Right then, here y'are," Laurie said, handing the youth a screwdriver.

Damon took the thing as if it were a spitting cobra. "If you're sure it's OK?" he said.

"Course it's OK," George chided him. "Me and Laurie've been doing it for years. Like I said, it's our only perk."

"A very nice perk too," Laurie grinned. "Just look at today's collection." He nodded towards a shelf against the far wall. Steve glanced that way and saw it contained gold rings, medallions, bracelets, even a Rolex watch. Then he realised these three were modern-day grave robbers. They searched the bodies for valuables. The notion of that would have amused him once. Now he felt a strange sense of outrage followed instantly by immense relief. Thankfulness swelled in his heart both celestial and otherwise.

164

Damon stepped up to the coffin and with a trembling hand he began to unscrew the lid. The job took longer than it ought, but at last he managed it.

The three realised as soon as the lid came up that Steve wasn't dead. They couldn't be unaware of it, with sweat greasing his face and his fingers twitching.

Damon almost leaped back, eyes bulging. "It's alive," he screamed.

Steve sent out a prayer of gratitude. He hadn't been abandoned after all.

George and Laurie puffed out their cheeks. "These shitty doctors and undertakers, they don't know their corpses from their arses," Laurie said with a shake of the head. He reached into the coffin, grasping Steve's wrist as if to feel for a pulse. But that wasn't his purpose. He only wanted to lift the hand so he could get at Steve's wedding ring more easily. After removing the ring, he dragged Steve's head forward so George could reach the clasp of his chunky gold-and-diamond chain.

"What the hell are you doing?" Steve yelled in his interworld where they couldn't hear. "Call an ambulance or someone to get me out of here."

Valuables removed, they dumped him back on his pillow and slammed down the coffin lid.

"What the *hell!*" Steve screamed.

"It's alive," Damon said again, supremely dull-witted. His jaw hung slack. "Aren't we going to tell someone?"

"Tell someone?" Laurie repeated as if mystified.

"You know, raise the alarm."

Sighing, the two men glanced at each other.

"Use your brains, son," George said to Damon as if talking to a child. "We've no choice but to burn him."

Burn me, for God's sake?

"The first time we found a live body we really did raise the alarm," Laurie said. "Claimed we opened the coffin because we heard a noise from inside. But we can't say that every time, can we?"

"Every time?" Damon repeated, face bloodless.

"It happens a few times every year," Laurie said. "Always some poor bugger paralysed but sweating like a pig. Now, we can't pretend they've *all* made a noise, can we? So how do we raise the alarm without admitting that we open every coffin as a matter of course?"

"Think about it, boy," George said.

With that the two men wheeled Steve's coffin to the vacant cremator and shoved it inside. Then they slammed the door. Its clang reverberated through the coffin and the body inside it, and through Steve's head on both sides of the veil. Other clangs followed as the other five cremators were sealed. Seconds later, gas ignited.

And then at last Steve found his voice. That is, the physical Steve – the one inside the coffin. He let out a yell. A howling, pleading screech. But no one heard him above the roaring gas jets.

The Name of the Star (Liam A. Spinage)

I write this missive in the understanding that whosoever discovers it may comprehend the summary of my research and then seek to repeat it, perhaps with more caution than I. The knowledge herein contains the secret name of the star which I believe to be unknown to the guild who would do everything in their power to obtain it. I shall start with a little history.

The liberator fell from a star.

Whatever shape it took, how it presented itself in its brief interactions with our people, is apparently lost to history. That may not be entirely accurate. It is equally likely that the guild is sitting on that information and not sharing it. That has happened a lot since the arrival of the liberator. Those who were present at the event - the oldest among us of whom precious few remain - have but the vaguest of memories which can be awakened only out of earshot of the guild and their network of spies. Even then, it often takes strong liquor or a hefty bribe of gold and I am currently lacking in both.

What happened then was this. The liberator is called such because the craft they arrived in happened to land - evidently accidentally - on the dwelling of the one who ruled in those days. That iron fist, that velvet glove, are now relics of our history. The craft of the liberator is not. It squats in the middle of the village, surrounded by a high fence of barbed wire and patrolled by agents of the guild who will not allow others to plunder its secrets. One tyranny was exchanged for another.

The guild moved quickly, once the liberator had left on their journey and left the craft behind. From the accounts I have managed to glean, and from stolen glances through the wire, it resembles one of our own dwellings, larger in size but fashioned similarly of wood. Whilst it is not whitewashed in our traditional fashion, the timbers are from trees not unknown to these parts. Curiosity compelled many in the early days to investigate the scene of our liberation, but the guild decided that the contents should only be studied by experts.

Their experts.

'KEEP OUT' signs were erected, guards were posted. Before his passing, my father used to tell me that several local households still had artifacts of the liberator they had themselves, in turn, liberated from the craft. These were held in high esteem, often placed in prominence on a table as a talking piece or given pride of place on a mantle for good luck. A few folk marveled at them, others sought to understand them. The guild sought only to suppress them. One night, their agents knocked down doors on every house where artifacts were said to dwell and confiscated the whole bunch. Their tyrannical takeover was complete, or so they thought.

That night, the resistance began, first in glances exchanged, then in whispers stolen, then in meetings held out of sight and out of mind. The guild always broke these up when they found out about them. Punishment for attendance was severe. The resistance faltered but did not die. What they did was begin to pray.

In hidden glades and lost caves, wherever the resistance met, they offered prayers to the liberator. They begged for another chance for freedoms they had neither the power nor courage to win themselves. What artifacts remained amongst the population were set on plinths and altars as objects of adulation and genuflection. Crude wooden replicas of the craft were fashioned in silence, left roofless so that when within, worshippers could gaze up at the night sky and hope, dream, pray for salvation. The stars, in their turn, merely twinkled in mute acceptance of their newfound supplicants.

Nothing came.

In more academic circles such as my father's - and now mine - there were heated discussions which went beyond the blind faith professed by the multitude. How had the craft arrived? From which star did it originate? Theories abounded, ideas debated and plans discarded. Eventually, these vague plans coalesced around a single sentiment: Could the star be reached? Then, in refinement, *how* could the star be reached? If the craft could make it here, what would it take for us to make the return journey? All of this was done in the hushed corners of libraries and without the benefit of those benefactors we had relied on in the past, all so that the guild would notice the activities taking place under their very noses.

Since it is forbidden to possess star charts of the night sky, we made them anew from scratch, from observation, from memory, hiding them in plain sight on the skins of paper lanterns which only illuminated them when they themselves were lit up. The star at the center of these charts was the one from which we believed the liberator had originated.

Tonight I will make that journey. It is a further distance by far than any of our people have ever traveled and yet this is the first time in many years that I feel totally unafraid.

I will leave my own cottage under cover of darkness, sure of my mission. Sneak past the guild guardsmen, their halberds crossed under the 'KEEP OUT' sign on the imposing gate before the craft of the liberator, the barbs of wire furled over it glistening in the low moonlight. Tiptoe my way to the far glade, beyond the road to the west. From there, I should be able to hear the resistance movement chanting in unison and pass between them as they call forth the name of the liberator in their throes of ecstasy: "Doh - roh - ti, Doh - roh - ti!" their intonations guttural, the words alien to my ears yet somehow comforting. I have watched this ceremony a thousand times and it always sets my senses on edge as they prostrate themselves before the facsimile of the craft which they face in worship.

I shall journey to that distant star and find another liberator to assist us. Else, I will become the liberator of that star, perhaps, and be placed among them as a king, to rule in benevolence rather than fear.

If you have found this, it is likely that I have not returned; lost on the long journey into the void of the heavens or in turbulent somnolence in the realms between dreams and nightmares. I know not which. I only beg, dear reader, that you continue my work. It is for this reason I leave you with the name of the star as spoken by the liberator.

"Kan-Zazz."

Meet the authors

Dorothy Davies is an editor, writer and medium. Somehow all these things come together in her seemingly crowded leisure and work life. She retired from editing for a while to run a second hand shop, the best one on the Isle of Wight, but the thrill of finding and publishing outstanding stories became too much so she started again with the Gravestone Press imprint. She has since closed the shop, here being other things to do... Her book, The Skullface Chronicles, the story of a zombie taking revenge on his dysfunctional family, is available through fiction4all.com. She has a box full of short stories, some of which are finding their way into the anthologies, having not seen daylight for many a long year. She also channels books from spirit authors, notable figures from our history. These can be found on the fiction4all.site under Zadkiel Publishing.

Paul Edwards is a life-long horror fan and writes his own twisted tales in any spare time that he can grab. He has seen three collections of stories published – *Now That I've Lost You* (Screaming Dreams), *Black Mirrors* (Rainfall Books) and *Night Voices* (Demain Publishing), the latter being a joint-collection with author Frank Duffy. Paul is also a fan of role-playing games, rock music and rough Somerset cider.

Jason R. Frei lives in Eastern Pennsylvania where he works as a therapist with children and adolescents. He writes speculative fiction culled from the experiences of his life and those he works with and blends science fiction, fantasy and horror into new creations. His flash story "The Garden" will be featured in the horror anthology 99 Tiny Terrors by Pulse Publishing and his short story "Some of the Parts" will be featured in the horror anthology Toilet Zone 3: The Royal Flush by Hellbound Books Publishing. Visit him online: https://facebook.com/odinstones.

Travis Mushanksi - was born and raised on the Canadian Prairies. He now works as a professional brewer in the craft beer industry. He graduated from the BA English program at the University of Regina where he focused on creative writing. Over the past ten years, he has worked as a freelance writer and editor for various online projects. He occasionally finds himself writing short fiction exploring the nightmares and horrors that hide just out of sight. Of course, all of this is possible because of the support of his wonderful wife, Janelle, and his beautiful daughter, Emma.

Victoria Nangle writes poetry and short stories, including the publication of the short poetry collection 'Nappers Delight & Other Short Poems' in the summer of 2022, as well as regularly writing and performing short stories at Brighton Horrorfest since 2019. She has been an arts journalist for 20 years and in 2019 the Komedia New Comedy

Award was launched in association with Victoria Nangle and the comedy club Comic Boom.

Rickey Rivers Jr. was born and raised in Alabama. He is a Best of the Net nominated writer and cancer survivor. His work has appeared in the JJ Outre Review, Stellium Literary Magazine, Fabula Argentea (among other publications).

Diane Arrelle has more than 350 short stories published and two short story collections: Just A Drop In The Cup and Seasons On The Dark Side. She, her sane husband and insane cat live on the edge of the New Jersey (USA) Pine Barrens (home of the Jersey Devil).

LaVern Spencer McCarthy has written and published five books of poetry and four books of dark fiction short stories. Her short stories have been featured in The Writers and Readers Magazine, Fresh Words Magazine, Fenechty Publications-Anthology of Short Stories, Writers Cache and many others. She resides in Blair Oklahoma.

Rie Sheridan Rose multitasks. A lot. Her short stories appear in numerous anthologies, including Killing It Softly Vol. 1 & 2, Hides the Dark Tower, Dark Divinations and On Fire. She has authored twelve novels, six poetry chapbooks and lyrics for dozens of songs. She is also editor-in-chief for Mocha Memoirs Press and editor for the Thirteen O' Clock imprint of Horrified Press. She tweets as @RieSheridanRose.